I0529423

Marcel is a spirit. Apparently, that doesn't mean he's dead, which he's more than a little grateful for. He's still stuck in ghost form, though, and he has no idea what happened or how to fix it.

Will never knew he was a psychic, but it looks like he's been seeing dead people without realizing it. Now he does, and he's going to use everything he can to help save Marcel, his best friend's brother.

But no one knows what happened to Marcel or where he is. Even when they realize someone has cast Marcel out of his body to steal his life energy, it doesn't put them closer to finding him.

They have limited time before Marcel's life energy is gone and he dies — for real this time.

The unauthorized reproduction or distribution of this copyrighted work is illegal. Criminal copyright infringement, including infringement without monetary gain, is investigated by the FBI and is punishable by up to 5 years in federal prison and a fine of $250,000.

This book is a work of fiction. Names, characters, places, and incidents either are products of the author's imagination or are used fictitiously. Any resemblance to actual events or locales or persons, living or dead, is entirely coincidental.

A Psychic of a Problem
Copyright © 2022 Catherine Lievens
ISBN: 978-1-4874-3300-0
Cover art by Angela Waters

All rights reserved. Except for use in any review, the reproduction or utilization of this work in whole or in part in any form by any electronic, mechanical or other means, now known or hereafter invented, is forbidden without the written permission of the publisher.

Published by eXtasy Books Inc

Look for us online at:
www.eXtasybooks.com

A Psychic of a Problem
It's a Psychic World 2

By

Catherine Lievens

CHAPTER ONE

Everything was dark. That was all Marcel could focus on, but he wanted out. He didn't know what was happening to him, and he didn't care. He wanted his brother, but the problem was that he didn't know how to get to him.

It was strange. Marcel couldn't feel anything, not even his body. He was afraid to open his eyes, afraid of what he'd see if he did.

What was happening to him?

He had no answers, and he wouldn't get them until he opened his eyes. He'd never been a coward, so he forced himself to do just that.

At first, he couldn't see anything. The darkness followed him, even when he tried to move. Then things started changing.

He could see a little bit of light, but not a lot. There was the outline of a house, but his eyes focused on a light coming out of it. He moved closer, needing to be out of the darkness.

The light was a man.

None of this made sense, but as long as Marcel stayed with the man, he wouldn't be in the darkness. That was all he cared about right now, so he made a beeline for the guy, hoping the guy wouldn't mind.

He stopped next to another object. It wasn't as big as the house, but when he tried to touch it to identify what it was, he couldn't.

His hand went right through it.

"Who is it?" someone asked, getting Marcel's attention.

"How am I supposed to know?" someone else answered. They were both men, from the sound of it, but Marcel couldn't identify either of them. He couldn't identify anything, and he was starting to panic.

What was wrong with him? Why couldn't he see anything? Why couldn't he touch anything?

"Maybe you should ask them," the first voice said.

"I don't think I'll have a choice." The first man moved closer. "Hi," he said.

Marcel blinked, trying to see better. He hadn't expected it to work, but to his surprise, it did. The car he'd been standing next to became more real, and while he still couldn't touch it when he tried, at least he knew it was a car now. "Hi. How did I get here?"

Marcel could see the man now. He was tall, with short blond curls and blue eyes. He was cute, but that wasn't the reason Marcel was here.

The problem was that Marcel didn't know where he was or why he was here. He didn't know anything, and he was starting to panic.

He swallowed. He needed his brother. Jerome would make everything better. He always did.

"I'm not sure," the cute man said. "Can you tell me the last thing you remember?"

Marcel hesitated. What *did* he remember? He honestly wasn't sure. He frowned as he thought, but the only thing that came to his mind was a room. There was a man there, but Marcel didn't feel much when he thought about the guy, so he didn't think he knew him.

The only thing he knew for sure was that he wanted his brother.

Marcel had never resented the fact that even though he was older than Jerome by one year, Jerome had always been the protector. It was ingrained in him for some reason, and

2

Marcel had always been more than happy to allow Jerome to keep him safe.

Not that he had needed him to. It wasn't like people attacked Marcel at every corner. But they were dragon shifters, and it wasn't an easy life, especially not when humans didn't know about them.

But Marcel was only sure of one thing right now. He wanted Jerome. Jerome would know what to do. He had to. "I don't know. A room. It was dark. I didn't know what was going on, and I wanted my brother."

The blond nodded. "That might be why you're here. Can you tell me your brother's name?"

What did the man mean when he said it might be why Marcel was here? Did the man know Jerome? Could he tell Marcel where to find him? "Jerome."

The blond sucked in a breath. "I'm sorry?"

"My brother's name. It's Jerome." That was what the man had been asking, right? He wanted to know Jerome's name, so Marcel had given it to him.

The man stared as if he'd seen a ghost. "And what's your name?"

"Marcel."

"What's going on?" The second voice asked, barely louder than a whisper.

Marcel frowned, a tingling of recognition telling him he was supposed to know who this person was.

"When did you hear from Marcel last?" the blond asked the other man, who was still invisible to Marcel.

"A few days ago. Why?"

"Because he's here. He's the ghost I'm talking to."

That got Marcel's attention. What did it mean? "Who are you?" he asked.

The blond looked frightened, which didn't make sense. Marcel was the one who was supposed to be scared. He had no idea what was going on, and when he tried to touch the car again, his hand went right through the door.

"My name is Lindsey," the blond said.

Marcel cocked his head. "Isn't that a woman's name?"

The blond's eyes narrowed. "It's my name, so clearly, it's not a woman's name." His expression shifted, and he looked at something Marcel knew he was supposed to see, too.

Why couldn't he?

"Can you tell me anything about your situation?" Lindsey asked. "What happened to you, where you are, how you feel. Anything can help."

Marcel raked a hand through his hair. "I don't know. What's going on?"

He felt like he was going nuts, and he didn't know how to stop. He was out of control, and he never was. Jerome was the protector, and Marcel was the control freak. That was how they worked. It had always been.

Lindsey raised his hands. "Don't panic."

Marcel huffed. "How am I supposed to do that? I don't know where I am or what's going on. I don't know why I can't touch the car or why I can't see anything beyond it and you. Wouldn't you be panicking if you were in my place?"

"I would. But panicking is only going to make things worse. Take a deep breath and try to relax. I think that the main reason you can't see much beyond me is that you're not really here."

"What does that mean?"

"I'm a psychic. I see ghosts."

Fear gripped Marcel's chest. "Am I dead?"

Lindsey hesitated, then shook his head. "I honestly don't know. You're not like any ghost I've ever dealt with, and I've dealt with a lot of them. I can't promise you're not dead, but I don't think so."

Jerome was going to kill Marcel—if he wasn't already

dead.

"Take a deep breath," Lindsey ordered.

Since he seemed to be the only one who knew what was going on, Marcel obeyed. He sucked in a breath, then another. It helped him relax, and it got even better when he closed his eyes. He focused on his breathing, hoping that whatever Lindsey was doing would help. He had to know what was going on, and he wouldn't if he didn't do what Lindsey said. That was one thing he was sure of. Whatever was going on, Lindsey seemed to have the answers, and Marcel wanted them.

"Good," Lindsey said after a moment. "Open your eyes now."

Marcel did, blinking. He hadn't expected anything to be different, so he was surprised to see he was standing in front of the house, right next to a car. He recognized the car now. It was Jerome's, and when Marcel looked around, he saw his brother.

Jerome looked horrible. His eyes were wide, and he was so pale that Marcel almost expected him to faint. He was hovering close to Lindsey, looking at Marcel, but Marcel suspected he couldn't actually see him.

"How are things now?" Lindsey asked.

Marcel nodded at him. "Better."

Lindsey opened his mouth, but Jerome stepped in before he could say anything. "What's going on?" he demanded to know.

His tone brought a smile to Marcel's lips. There was his brother, all right.

"I honestly don't know, but I think we should take this somewhere else," Lindsey said. "I don't think my grandmother and my father care if we do this here, but I don't want one of the neighbors to see."

Jerome nodded. "We can move, but can he travel?"

Marcel was almost offended that his brother was talking about him as if he wasn't there, but it made sense if he couldn't see Marcel. It was the only thing that did, and Marcel felt like he usually did when he felt a headache coming on.

Could he get headaches if he was dead?

"I'd like you to try to come with us in the car," Lindsey said.

Marcel didn't have to think before he nodded. "I'll come with you." He had no idea what was going on, but even if Lindsey couldn't help him, he wanted to be with his brother. Whatever was happening, Jerome would know what to do.

Or at least, Marcel prayed he would.

Will was cursing paperwork when he heard a noise. He frowned, listening and wondering if it was Jerome. His best friend had always worked late until recently. Now that he'd met Lindsey, he spent more time with his boyfriend than at the office, but Will didn't berate him for that. He'd do the same if he had a boyfriend.

But he didn't, which was why he was working tonight instead of going home. There was also the fact that he hated paperwork and always left it to the last moment.

The sound of the front door opening told him Jerome was here. Will had locked the door before getting to work, and the only other person who had a key was his best friend.

He got to his feet, wincing when his neck cracked as he turned his head. Was he already getting old at the age of thirty-four?

Glad for the interruption, he made his way to the front of the office. Lindsey and Jerome were in the waiting area, but they weren't alone. Will smiled when he saw Marcel. "Hey," he said. "I didn't expect the two of you to come back to the office tonight. I certainly didn't expect you to bring your brother along. How are you doing, Marcel?"

The answering silence was so thick that Will could almost feel it. The three were staring at him, making him nervous.

He chuckled. "What?"

"You can see him?" Lindsey asked.

"See who?"

"Marcel. You can see him?"

"Of course I can. What's going on?"

"How can you see him?" Jerome asked.

Will had the impression he was missing something, and whatever that something was, it was huge. "I didn't know Marcel was in town," he said slowly. "Is that why you're surprised?" But Lindsey and Jerome sounded surprised that Will could actually see Marcel, which didn't make sense.

Unless they couldn't.

"You can't see him?" he asked, fear gripping his stomach.

"I can," Lindsey answered. "But Jerome can't."

Lindsey was a psychic, which could mean only one thing. "He's dead?" Will asked in a whisper.

How could Marcel be dead? What happened to him?

"We don't know," Lindsey answered. "I can see him, while Jerome can't, so he could be, but I don't think that's the case. He's not like any other ghost I've ever dealt with. Something is wrong, but I don't know what it is."

"How can you be sure he's not dead?"

"I can't. I'm honestly not sure of anything right now, but I'm holding on to the hope that he's not dead and that's why he's different."

Will nodded. That was what they all needed to focus on. "Okay, so, if he's not dead, what's happening to him?"

"I have no idea. I also have no idea why you can see him."

Will hadn't thought of that. "I don't know. I've never seen ghosts before. Maybe it's because he's not a ghost?"

"But I should be able to see him, then," Jerome said with a

growl.

Will knew his friend. Jerome was frustrated, and that never ended well. Jerome always needed to be on the move and try to solve his problems. It didn't look like there was anything he could do at the moment, so he was no doubt going to start growling at everything and snapping at everyone. That was never pleasant, but especially not when they needed to focus on finding a solution to this problem, whatever it was.

"You've never seen ghosts?" Lindsey asked.

He was staring at Will as if he were a bug under a microscope. The only reason Will wasn't offended was that he knew Lindsey. He was wondering what was going on, and so was Will. "Not that I know of. Are ghosts very different from alive human beings?"

"It can be easy to mix them up, actually," Lindsey said. "They tend to act like they did when they were human, and some of them don't realize they're dead. It's when they realize that other people can see them that you can be sure some people are ghosts."

"So I might be able to see them?"

Lindsey shrugged. "Anything is possible. I've never heard about a psychic not realizing he saw ghosts, but I suppose it wouldn't be that surprising, especially if those ghosts never realized you were a psychic. That's another easy way to know they're ghosts. Once they realize you can see them, they make pests out of themselves." He turned to Marcel. "What do you see when you see him?" he asked.

Will knew Lindsey was asking him, so he stepped closer. Marcel looked uncomfortable, but he stayed where he was as Will looked him over.

Will frowned. "It's strange."

"What's strange? Just describe what you see," Lindsey pushed.

Will swallowed. He had no clue what was going on, and it

made him nervous. He wanted answers, but he didn't know if he'd get them. Lindsey didn't seem to know what was going on any more than him.

He stared at Marcel for a moment. "He's not quite right. It's the colors. He doesn't look as solid as he should."

Lindsey nodded. "Exactly."

"He's almost like an old picture. You know, the ones that start losing their color after a while? He's faded, if that makes sense."

"Nothing makes sense at the moment. That's how I see him, too."

Jerome huffed. "You never told me you were a psychic," he said, glaring at Will.

Will had to press his lips together so he wouldn't smile. "I don't know that I am. I've never seen ghosts."

"But you can see my brother, just like Lindsey, while I can't. That has to mean you're a psychic. We could have used your ability this entire time instead of looking for psychics to work with us."

Lindsey put his hands on his hips and glared at his boyfriend. "Does that mean you regret meeting me?"

Jerome's eyes widened. "That's not what I said."

"It's what you implied, though."

"I'm sorry. I didn't mean to. I suppose I'm stunned to find out that my best friend is a psychic."

But no one was as stunned as Will.

Could he be a psychic? He'd never seen ghosts, or at least, he didn't think so. Could it be as simple as Lindsey had said? Maybe Will had been seeing ghosts all along but hadn't realized it.

Will wanted to find out more about all of this, but they had other things to focus on right now. "So Marcel isn't a ghost," he said.

Lindsey sighed. "I don't think so, but I can't be sure of

anything. He's not like any other ghost I've ever dealt with, but I don't have that much experience. You know I tended to run away from ghosts before."

Because with no training, Lindsey couldn't keep them at bay. That meant ghosts tried taking advantage of him, and it usually wasn't pretty. Since Lindsey had started working with Jerome and Will, he'd seen what happened when Lindsey didn't do what a ghost wanted. It usually resulted in a temper tantrum from the ghost and Lindsey getting a headache.

Will kind of hoped he wasn't a psychic.

"What's going on?" he asked.

"We don't know," Jerome said. "The only thing we know is that Marcel suddenly appeared to Lindsey. Lindsey can see him, while I can't, which I thought meant he was dead. Now that Lindsey has explained how different Marcel is, though, we're not sure anymore."

Will looked at Marcel. He seemed lost in his thoughts, and, just like before, like he wasn't quite here. Will wondered what would happen if he tried touching Marcel. Marcel looked so faded that it was easy to imagine that Will's hand would go right through him.

He hoped Marcel wasn't dead. He'd grown up with Jerome and Marcel, and while they were both a few years older than him, the three of them had always been friends. Will was closer to Jerome, but it didn't mean he didn't want Marcel to be safe.

The problem was that no one knew what was going on, so how could they make sure Marcel was okay? And if Marcel wasn't dead, what was happening to him?

They didn't have answers, and Will had no idea where to start looking for them.

Marcel didn't feel dead, although he didn't exactly have any-thing to compare, since he'd never died. What did being dead feel like?

Jerome staggered to one of the chairs lining the wall and sat down. Marcel didn't want Jerome to be hurt.

He went to crouch in front of Jerome. Lindsey and Will could see Marcel, but Jerome obviously couldn't. because he didn't react when Marcel tried to look him in the eyes. It was as if Marcel wasn't even there, and he supposed that to Je-rome, he wasn't.

Lindsey cleared his throat. Marcel tried to ignore the pity on his face, but it wasn't easy.

"What's the last thing you remember?" Lindsey asked.

Marcel straightened with a sigh. His brother couldn't see him, but it didn't mean he wouldn't try to help. Jerome wouldn't let Marcel down, and neither would Will. Marcel didn't know Lindsey yet, but Jerome had told him about his boyfriend, and if Jerome trusted Lindsey, so did Marcel.

"I don't know. I already told you everything I remember. It's like there's a black hole where my memories should be."

Lindsey nodded as if he wasn't surprised. "How big is that hole? If you think, what's the last thing you remember? It doesn't need to have anything to do with your situation. I'm just trying to understand what we're dealing with."

Marcel sat in the chair next to Jerome. He was half sur-prised he didn't fall through the chair, but then he didn't know how ghosts worked. He didn't want to find out, either. He wasn't dead, or at least, that was what he kept trying to convince himself.

He closed his eyes and focused. Whatever the last memory Marcel could remember was, it probably had to do with the situation he was in now.

"I had a date," Marcel said.

That, he remembered. He'd met the guy at a coffee shop,

and they'd gotten talking. He'd been nice, and when Marcel asked him on a date, he'd said yes. Marcel couldn't say sparks had been flying between them, but it had been nice enough that Marcel had wanted to see if things could progress between them. He'd decided that if they wouldn't, he could still be friends with the guy.

"Who were you going out with?" Lindsey asked.

"A guy named York. I met him at a coffee shop. We chatted, and he said yes when I asked him out."

"Where were you meeting?"

"We had dinner. Thai, even though it's not my favorite. York enjoyed it, though."

"You remember dinner?"

Marcel did. He'd liked York even after dinner was over, and he'd been planning on asking if they could see each other again. "Do you want to know what we ate?"

"I don't think that's important. I'd like you to focus on York."

Marcel nodded. "He's in his early twenties."

"How early twenties? Around twenty? Maybe twenty-five?"

Jerome softly snorted. "Robbing the cradle?" he asked.

Marcel opened his eyes to glare at his brother, even though Jerome couldn't see it. "He's twenty-two, and age doesn't matter."

"I agree," Lindsey said. Jerome could see *his* glare, and while that wasn't as satisfying as glaring himself, it helped Marcel relax.

He might not know what was going on, but he wasn't facing this alone.

"You realize I don't know what he just said, right?" Jerome asked.

Lindsey sighed. "This is going to become complicated, and fast. He said that age doesn't matter."

Jerome shrugged. "I disagree, but I'll keep my mouth shut. I want to know what happened to him."

Lindsey reached for Jerome. Jerome took his boyfriend's hand and kissed the palm, and Marcel had to look away.

He was glad his brother had found someone and that he was so obviously happy, but at the moment, he had a hard time focusing on anything that wasn't him. He was worried he'd never be able to find out what happened, and even though Lindsey didn't think he was dead, it wouldn't help if he didn't find out what he was.

"Tell me more about York," Lindsey ordered. He and Jerome were still holding hands.

"I don't know him very well, to be honest. That's why we were on a date. He's blond, with brown eyes and freckles. He's shorter than you but taller than me."

"Do you know where we can find him?"

"I have his phone number, but I don't think I have my phone."

Marcel patted his pockets, just to make sure, but he couldn't feel it.

"So we don't have a way to contact him."

"You might be able to if you go to that coffee shop, but I'm not sure whether he was a regular or not. I don't know how to find him without his phone number." And since he was the last thing Marcel remembered, that might be a problem.

Lindsey leaned closer to Jerome and started quietly explaining what Marcel had said. Marcel looked away, wanting to give them privacy but also needing a little time to himself. When he turned, though, it was to find Will staring at him.

"So you're a psychic?" he asked.

Will had been Jerome's best friend since the three of them were children. He was three years younger than Marcel, but that had never stopped them from playing together first, then, once they were teenagers, from hanging out. Will had always been closer to Jerome, but Marcel liked him, and he considered Will a friend.

Will shrugged. "I have no idea."

"Since you can see me, it looks like you are. How do you feel about that?"

Will wrinkled his nose. "That it would have saved us a lot of problems if I'd realized that sooner. How didn't I? *That's* what I don't understand."

"I wouldn't know. I've never seen a ghost." And now, he was one.

"What happened after dinner?" Jerome asked.

"We left the restaurant," Marcel said slowly, trying to remember every detail he could. "We walked down the street. We were talking, but York seemed nervous."

"Why was he nervous?" Lindsey asked.

"I don't know. Maybe because we were done with dinner and he wasn't sure what would happen next? I'd already told him it was only dinner, but I guess that some guys are assholes."

"We agree on that. What happened next?"

"I remember walking for a bit. I'd picked him up, and I was planning on taking him home. We went to my car, but something happened." Marcel frowned. "I don't know what. The only thing I can remember is that I was talking to York and that everything went black. I'm sure I'm missing something."

Lindsey didn't look surprised. "People usually do when they die."

"So you think I'm dead?"

Lindsey hesitated. "I want to say no, but I can't be a hundred percent sure, and I don't want to give anyone false hope."

"But if I'm not dead, what happened to me?"

"I have no idea. I've never seen anything like this, but you have to remember I'm not trained. The only person who tried to teach me was my grandmother, and she wasn't quite sure where to start. She's not as strong a psychic as I am. I have no formal training, which is why I've always tried blocking out the ghosts. It never worked well, so I'm happy I don't have to anymore, but unfortunately, it doesn't help in this situation."

"You have to find a teacher," Jerome said.

"That would be for the best. If anything, I think that someone more experienced than me would be able to tell us what's happening to Marcel."

And Marcel wanted to know. He prayed he wasn't dead, but how could he be sure? And if he wasn't, what was happening to him? How did he get out of this situation?

Lindsey didn't have experience, but Will had even less. He still wanted to do something, but where should he start? Was there even anything he could do? He didn't want to make things worse, and they didn't know if Marcel was alive.

God, Will hoped he was.

"I know you don't want to make a mess, but do you think he's dead?" Jerome asked.

There was so much pain in his voice that Will wanted to hug him. Jerome had Lindsey now, though, and the psychic stepped in, moving closer to Jerome and wrapping his arms around him. "I could be wrong, but I don't think so," he said. "I've dealt with a lot of dead people, and none of them have been like him."

"What's happening to me, then?" Marcel asked.

He looked just as lost as Jerome. Will reached for him instinctively, but his hand went right through Marcel's thigh.

He and Marcel stared at the spot as Will cradled his hand to his chest. It hadn't hurt. In truth, he hadn't felt anything. It was just a reminder that something was happening to Marcel and that no one knew what.

"What now, then?" Jerome asked.

He was gearing himself up and no doubt reminding himself that he was supposed to protect Marcel. He'd failed, and now, he had to find a solution.

Will disagreed with the fact that it was Jerome's job to protect his brother, but he'd stopped trying to make Jerome see that a long time ago. Jerome treated him the same way, as if he were a younger brother that needed protection. Both he and Marcel were adults, but Jerome didn't seem to care. He wanted to protect them, and he'd do everything he could to make that happen.

Lindsey scratched his chin. "Well, I was planning on calling a guy I know."

"What guy?" Jerome asked.

"I don't *really* know him. I've been hanging around psychic forums for the past few weeks. I was trying to find out if someone could help me learn since I took this job and everything. I got a name, but while we chatted a bit, I haven't actually met the guy."

"And you trust him?"

"I don't know. He hasn't done or said anything that would make him untrustworthy in my eyes, but I could be wrong. The problem is that we need help, and he knows what he's talking about when it comes to being a psychic and ghosts. I think he's our best bet."

Jerome didn't look convinced, and to be honest, neither was Will. How were they supposed to know that this guy could help them? "There's no one else?" he asked, hoping Lindsey would suddenly remember someone else, someone they could trust.

But Lindsey shook his head. "If I knew anyone else who could help, I'd have learned how to deal with ghosts a long time ago. I trust Victor, though, as much as I can trust someone I've never met face to face. I truly think he can help us."

Jerome and Will looked at each other. It was obvious from Jerome's expression that he wanted to say no, but he was also aware that this Victor might be their only way to help Marcel.

"He offered to train me, so he won't be surprised when I ask to meet him," Lindsey continued.

Jerome got to his feet. "Fine. I agree with this only because it seems it's the only way to help Marcel. I'll be there when you meet Victor, though."

"I had no doubt you would be."

Jerome's eyes narrowed. "And you're not going to argue? To tell me that you can do this by yourself and that you're not a child?"

Will looked away. He couldn't help the smile on his lips. When his two friends were like that, it was easy to remember how they'd been at each other's throats when they'd first met. Jerome had wanted nothing to do with a human, and he'd hurt Lindsey when he'd said it to his face. Lindsey had wanted the job, though, and he was stubborn as hell. He'd stayed, and he and Jerome had fought every step of the way, at least until they'd ended up in bed. It was good to see them like this, even if only for a moment. It brought familiarity to a situation where nothing else was.

Will's gaze crossed with Marcel's, and they smiled at each other. Marcel had never seen Jerome and Lindsey together, but it was obvious he found their interaction amusing.

"I'm going to call him," Lindsey said.

He stepped to the side of the room, his phone already in his hand. Jerome came toward Will, and Will was relieved he didn't sit in the chair his brother was in.

"You never told me you could see ghosts," Jerome said.

Will rolled his eyes. Of course that was what Jerome wanted to talk about. For now, there was nothing he could do to help Marcel, so he'd focus on Will instead. "I would have told you if I'd known I could."

Jerome looked down at Will. "How is that possible?"

"I don't know. I don't even know if I have psychics in the family. I've never realized that some of the people I saw around were dead, but I'm glad I didn't."

Will had heard enough from Lindsey about how some ghosts behaved. He wasn't exactly happy about being able to see them and communicate with them. He was glad for it because it meant he could communicate with Marcel, but beyond that, he couldn't say he was looking forward to having to deal with it.

Jerome looked around as if looking for his brother. He probably was. "What do you think about Marcel's situation?" he asked.

"Since I didn't know I could see dead people until now, I doubt that anything I can think of about the situation would be helpful."

"Humor me."

Jerome wanted to be distracted, something Will could understand. He looked at Marcel, who'd closed his eyes but was probably listening to the conversation. "I hope he's not dead. I don't want him to be."

"Neither do I. I hate that I can't do anything to help him."

"You're doing everything you can at the moment."

Jerome snorted. "If I was doing everything I could, I'd be out there finding a solution."

"But don't you see? You might not know what to do about it, but you're working on it, and, more importantly, you're there for him. A lot of people would have run the other way, but you haven't."

Jerome made a disgusted sound. "Those people don't deserve my brother."

"Just be there for him. You can't see him, but he can see you, and he can hear you. Why do you think he appeared to Lindsey?"

"I don't know." Jerome frowned. "He doesn't know Lindsey."

"But Lindsey knows *you*. I might be talking out of my ass right now, but I truly believe that he found Lindsey because he was looking for you. He didn't appear to your parents or to his best friend. He appeared to Lindsey, your boyfriend."

Jerome nodded and looked around. "I'll do everything I can to help you," he promised.

When Will caught his eye, he tilted his chin toward the chair Marcel was sitting in. Jerome nodded and turned his attention to his brother, and since Lindsey was still on the phone, it left Will on his own for a moment.

He rubbed his face. He was exhausted, which he supposed didn't help with the situation. Still, he couldn't believe he was a psychic and that he hadn't realized it for all these years. He was thirty-four, for fuck's sake. Shouldn't he have noticed he could see dead people before now?

"He's coming," Lindsey said.

Will turned to find that he wasn't on the phone anymore.

"When?" Jerome asked.

"As soon as possible, in the next few days. He has to take time off work, but he wants to help."

"And you trust him?"

Lindsey sighed. "As much as I can trust someone I've never met. I'm not even entirely sure he can help us, but he's willing to try, and at the moment, that's all that matters, isn't it?"

Will supposed he wasn't wrong. As much as he didn't want to trust someone he didn't know, Lindsey's friend was the only person who could help them. Hopefully, he would.

Will didn't know what they'd do if he couldn't.

CHAPTER TWO

Marcel liked Lindsey. He hadn't been sure initially, although he realized now it was because of their situation. Marcel had been confused and scared. And while Lindsey had been trying to help, he hadn't been able to do anything useful except call his friend, who still hadn't arrived. But Marcel had been spending time with Lindsey and Jerome, and he'd gotten to know Lindsey over the past few days. It would have been hard for him not to, considering Lindsey and Will were the only two people in Marcel's life who could see him and talk to him right now.

In the beginning, it had been hard to understand why Lindsey and Jerome were together. They were in love and behaved like they were, but they also constantly snapped at each other and bickered. Marcel had wondered if maybe they were about to break up, but the more time he spent with them, the more he realized it was just how they were. They showed their love for each other through kisses and touches, but also by bickering, and they both seemed to enjoy it. Marcel didn't understand it, but he supposed he didn't have to. He wasn't the one dating Lindsey, after all.

He was even enjoying spending time with Jerome, although that was harder. Jerome couldn't see or hear him, and it made having a conversation complicated. It was easier when Lindsey and Will were present, but they couldn't spend their time repeating what Marcel was saying.

Marcel sighed and looked at the ceiling of the guest room. He was staying with Jerome and Lindsey, and it was almost time to go to work. He had to admit he couldn't wait. As much as he enjoyed spending time with his brother and Lindsey, it was also good to see Will. They'd always been friendly, and it was nice to have someone else to talk to. Lindsey was great, but he was more focused on Jerome than Marcel, which made sense. He was worried for Jerome.

Marcel was, too, maybe even more than he was for himself. Whatever was happening to him, he wasn't in pain. Whether or not he was dead, there was nothing he could do to change his situation. He could try to help his brother, though. He doubted Jerome would be okay until they found out what happened to him, especially since it was obvious Jerome felt guilty about not being there for Marcel.

It didn't matter how many times Marcel had Lindsey or Will tell Jerome it wasn't his fault. He was still convinced this wouldn't have happened if he'd been there, and Marcel didn't know how to make him change his mind.

He got up. As far as he'd been able to see, he couldn't touch anything, which meant that getting breakfast ready was out. He didn't want to stay in bed, though. Staring at the ceiling didn't help, and he had enough of it. He'd wait for Lindsey and Jerome to be ready in the living room or the kitchen.

Since he was maybe dead, maybe not, Marcel didn't need to use the bathroom. He also didn't need to shower, so he left the guest room and went straight to the kitchen.

He regretted it as soon as he stepped foot inside.

Lindsey was on his stomach on the table, both hands grabbing one of the edges. His feet were on the ground, his lower body naked. Jerome was behind him, and, from the way he moved and his jeans around his ankles, what he was doing was obvious.

Marcel slammed his eyes shut and stepped back, not wanting to see any more of that. He was pretty sure Lindsey hadn't seen him, but he didn't know if he'd ever be able to look the man in the eyes again without blushing and making it obvious that he'd seen something he shouldn't have.

He retreated back to his guestroom, but he couldn't get the image of his brother fucking his boyfriend out of his mind. Where was brain bleach when he needed it?

Was this something that would happen regularly? Jerome and Lindsey hadn't been together long, so it made sense they were still in the honeymoon phase. It wasn't even surprising that they'd forgotten Marcel was hanging around the place. Marcel hoped he wouldn't have to see it again, but he also wanted to be proactive about it.

Lindsey wasn't the only person Marcel could talk to. There was Will, too, and hopefully, he didn't have a new boyfriend hanging around his apartment. Marcel didn't think Will would say no if Marcel asked if he could stay with him, and now that he'd seen what he'd seen, he couldn't wait.

He wasn't sure how long he stayed in his bedroom, but after a while, there was a hesitant knock on the door. He groaned and sat up, calling out, "Yes?"

The door opened, and Lindsey peeked in. He looked sheepish, and his expression was enough to tell Marcel he'd seen him when he'd walked into the kitchen.

"Sorry about that," Lindsey said, rubbing the back of his neck.

"It's fine. This is your home, and it makes sense that you're not used to having someone staying with you."

"It's not because you're a ghost. We did the same thing at work the other week, and Will was appalled."

Marcel laughed. Unfortunately for him, he now could too easily imagine what Will had walked in on. "I think I'll be staying with Will from now on," he said.

"You don't have to. I promise we'll keep this to the bedroom from now on."

Marcel got off the bed. "It's fine. I don't expect you to

change your entire life because I'm around. Unless Will has a new boyfriend?"

"He hasn't told me anything," Lindsey said as he and Marcel walked back to the kitchen. "I don't think he's seeing anyone at the moment. But you don't have to move out."

Jerome's face was bright red when Marcel met him in the kitchen. He stared at the corner of the room, but Marcel didn't know if it was because he didn't want to look at him or because he didn't know where he was exactly.

"I'm really sorry about that," Jerome said.

"Tell him it doesn't matter and that I'm moving in with Will, please," Marcel told Lindsey. Lindsey repeated the message, but Marcel wasn't done. "Please, also tell him I'm happy for him and for you. I've always wanted to see him fall in love with a good person, and he did."

Lindsey was smiling as he told Jerome what Marcel had just said. He guided Jerome until he was in front of Marcel, looking straight at him this time.

"I've never been as happy as I am with Lindsey," Jerome said. "And I know you'll find the same thing soon."

"Being invisible to most people is going to make it hard to date," Marcel said with a smile.

"That just means we'll have to find out what happened to you and fix it soon," Lindsey said. There was a stubborn tilt to his chin that told Marcel he'd do everything he could to do just that.

It was good not to be alone to face this, especially since Marcel had no idea what was going on. They still weren't even sure whether or not he was dead, but Marcel had hope. If there was anyone who could find out and help him, it was Jerome and Will, and now, Lindsey.

Marcel might not know Lindsey well, but Jerome wouldn't be with him if Lindsey wasn't a good person. Marcel trusted him as much as he trusted Jerome and Will. He didn't know what he'd do if they couldn't fix this, but he wasn't going to think about it right now. He couldn't lose hope, not when it was the only thing they had working for them at the moment.

Will was supposed to be at work, but this morning, he had something else to do—namely, talk to his parents about being a psychic.

He didn't think either of his parents were psychics, but maybe they knew about someone in the family. Knowing who it was likely wouldn't change anything, but it would make Will feel better. At least, he'd know where the gift came from.

Although from listening to Lindsey, it sounded more like a curse than a gift. So far, Will hadn't had any problem with it, but he'd just found out.

He knocked on his parents' door and waited for someone to answer. It was early still, but they'd always been early birds. He knew they'd be awake, probably in the kitchen having coffee.

It took a moment for his father to answer. When he did, he frowned and looked around as if expecting Will to have someone with him.

"What are you doing here so early in the morning?" he asked as he stepped aside to let Will in. "And where's Jerome? You two are usually attached at the hip."

Will smiled. "Not since he's found a boyfriend."

"Has he? What about you?"

Will rolled his eyes. "You're worse than Mom when it comes to gossip."

"It's not gossip. I just want my son to be happy."

For some reason, Will's thoughts flashed to Marcel. He couldn't think about having a boyfriend while Marcel was still in the state he was in. They didn't even know if he was dead, for fuck's sake. "I don't need a boyfriend to be happy," he told his father as they walked to the kitchen.

His father patted his shoulder. "I know that. Sorry if I was pushy."

"You weren't. But Jerome is happy with Lindsey, and that's why he's not spending as much time with me. Besides, he's also dealing with his brother at the moment." Will wouldn't tell his parents what the problem was with Marcel exactly, but they knew him, so he could tell them that much at least.

"Well, tell him we're happy for him. We can't wait to meet the lucky guy."

"You'll love Lindsey. As soon as things calm down at work, I'll arrange something so we can have dinner together."

Just like Will had expected, his mother was in the kitchen, sitting at the breakfast table sipping coffee. She seemed surprised to see him, but she smiled. "To what do we owe the honor of your presence?" she asked as he kissed her cheek.

He rolled his eyes and flopped into what had been his chair until he left home. "Honor, huh?"

"We don't often get to see you these days, especially not at this hour of the day. Or is there a problem?"

"Not a problem, exactly. I just needed to ask you something."

"What is it?" she asked, leaning closer.

Will waited until his father was done pouring him a cup of coffee. He didn't know how his parents would react to this. Maybe they'd brush what Will could do off and tell him psychics didn't exist. That was what most humans would do, and his parents hadn't been deep in the supernatural world for most of their lives like Will had. They knew about Jerome and Marcel because it had been impossible for them not to find out when they were kids, but as far as Will knew, that was all they were aware of when it came to that world.

He tapped his fingertips on the table. "You know about

dragon shifters," he started.

His mother blinked. "Of course we do."

"Have you ever wondered if there was more to the world than just dragon shifters?"

His mother snorted. "We're very much aware of the fact that there's more to the world than them. What's this about? Stop beating around the bush and tell us."

"Jerome's new boyfriend is a psychic. That means he sees ghosts while the rest of the world doesn't."

"Like my grandmother," Will's father said.

Will blinked at him. "Your grandmother?"

"Yes. Well, that's what everyone in the family says about her, anyway. I don't remember her well. I was very young when she passed away." He took a sip of coffee. "But the stories in the family are that she could see ghosts."

Will groaned and rubbed his face. "You never thought about telling me?"

"I never really thought about it. Why?"

"Well, it turns out that I might be a psychic, too."

His parents stared at him for a moment. "What does it mean?" his mother asked eventually. "Are you okay?"

Will couldn't help but smile. Of course it was the first thing his mother worried about. "I'm fine. I just didn't expect this to happen."

"Neither did I, or I'd have told you," his father said. "Can you tell us what's going on?"

"Just that now that Lindsey is working with Jerome and me, we've been talking, and the last time he saw someone who wasn't supposed to be there, I saw them, too." This was the best way to tell them what happened without actually telling them about Marcel.

"And you're sure this person was a ghost?"

"We haven't had the time to sit down and talk about what this means, but it seems like I might be a psychic."

"I had no idea this was a possibility," Will's father said. "I'm sorry I never thought about telling you. Will you be okay?"

"I think so, especially since someone is coming to teach Lindsey how to control this gift. I'll take lessons, too." Will suspected he was going to need them.

Will couldn't help but wonder why this gift had decided to surface only now, or if maybe he'd had it the entire time but had never realized it. Whatever the case, it would come in handy in some cases he worked with Jerome. It was good to have Lindsey with them, but having two psychics would be even better.

His father told Will a bit about his grandmother, and while Will was interested, it was nothing he could use at the moment. He left after breakfast, headed to the office. He wanted to check in on Marcel and make sure he was okay.

He doubted that was the case. How could anyone in Marcel's situation be fine? Will would be going nuts if it were him, and he wanted to do everything he could to get Marcel out of trouble.

Because there was no way he wasn't in trouble. Whatever had happened to him shouldn't have, and it was a problem.

He was surprised to see the others were already there when he got to the office. These days, Jerome and Lindsey always arrived after him, no doubt because they had something better to do in the morning.

Will grimaced. "Have you traumatized Marcel yet?" he asked as he walked into the tiny room they used as a break room. He knew that was where he'd find them, probably sipping coffee.

Marcel was sitting on the edge of the couch, and he grimaced when he heard Will's question. "Kitchen table," he said.

Will chuckled. "Better than the couch you're sitting on."

Marcel jumped off the couch as if it had bitten him. Will laughed until he saw Lindsey's face. The man's cheeks were so red that he looked like he was about to explode. Jerome, on the other hand, looked amused as he sipped his cup of coffee while leaning against the table.

"We already apologized for that," he told Will.

"You did, but it's still a couch we were all supposed to use. How am I supposed to sit on it now?"

"Can we not talk about this? This morning has already been awkward enough."

"So I've heard." And Will wasn't surprised Marcel had walked in on them. Their relationship was still new, and they were going at it like bunnies. Will didn't blame them, but he did blame them for where they did it, especially at work. "I went to see my parents this morning."

Lindsey frowned. "Why? Has something happened?"

"No. I just wanted to ask them about me being a psychic. Apparently, my grandmother on my father's side could see ghosts, too."

"So it explains why you have this gift."

"But not why I've never seen ghosts before. How does that work? If I have this gift, didn't I have it the entire time? Why did I never see ghosts until now?"

"You probably saw them but never realized it," a voice said behind him.

Jerome quickly put himself between Lindsey and the man who'd arrived, but Marcel stayed where he was. It wasn't like there was anything he could do, anyway. He was a ghost.

But he didn't miss the way Will placed himself between him and the man. He had to know no one could hurt Marcel at the moment, but he was still thinking about protecting him, and it did something to Marcel.

"Who are you?" Jerome asked with a growl. "How did you get in?"

The man smiled. "I apologize. I knocked, but no one answered, and the door was open. When I heard voices, I decided to follow them. My name is Victor."

He offered Jerome his hand. Jerome stared for a moment as if it might bite him but eventually shook it. Victor moved on to Lindsey, then to Will, who had relaxed.

"As I was saying, you probably saw ghosts but never realized it," he said as they shook hands, too. "It's not as uncommon as you might think. Ghosts are tough to tell apart from humans, although with training, you'll be able to do it." He smiled. "Either that or your gift isn't very strong, which is also something we can work on if you wish." He stepped away from Will and turned to Marcel. "And you're the reason I'm here."

Marcel offered Victor his hand automatically, only to drop it a second later. "Yeah, that would be me. I'd shake your hand, but I'm sure you can see how that's impossible."

Victor was staring at Marcel as if he were an interesting experiment. Marcel supposed he was, but that didn't mean he had to like it.

"I do see," Victor confirmed. "It's interesting."

Marcel scoffed. "I wouldn't call it interesting." He'd call it horrifying, or maybe terrifying. He felt both those emotions.

"You're clearly not human at the moment, yet, you're also not a ghost," Victor said as he cocked his head and continued staring.

"You know what happened to me? Am I dead?"

"I understand how that's your main worry."

"Can you tell me if I'm dead, then?" Because if he was, Marcel wanted to know. He wanted to start making his peace with it, and he wouldn't be able to until he was sure of it.

Victor stared at him for a moment longer. "I don't believe you are."

"You don't believe it, or you know I'm not dead?" Marcel asked.

"You're not dead."

Marcel's shoulders slumped in relief. Since he wasn't dead, there was still a chance he could fix whatever this was. He'd been sure Victor would tell him he was a ghost now, but he hadn't wanted to deal with it. Now, he wouldn't have to.

He still had to deal with the fact that he wasn't in his body anymore. Or maybe he was, and this was what his body was like? He didn't know, but he'd like some answers.

"We should probably sit down for this," Lindsey intervened.

Victor turned his attention to him. "It's a pleasure to meet you, Lindsey. I wasn't sure you'd want to, even after we talked."

Marcel wanted to shake Victor and ask him to do *something*, but he wanted this man to help him. It probably wouldn't be for the best to start yelling at him.

Lindsey poured Victor a cup that was more sugar than coffee. Once they were all sitting around the tiny table except for Marcel, who didn't fancy having someone spear their elbow into his invisible stomach, silence fell on the room. It was slightly awkward, and Marcel wanted to break it, but he wasn't sure how. Should he get straight to the point once again?

"How do you know about this?" Jerome asked, waving his hand at the room.

Victor leaned back in his chair. "I'm a psychic, and it's a family thing. My father is a psychic, as is his mother. I'm told my great-grandmother was one, too. It's a gift passed down from generation to generation, and in my family, it means we're taught how to deal with it from a young age. My brothers had to learn, too, although one of them can't see ghosts as far as we know."

"My grandmother has a bit of the gift, but it's always been easier for her to ignore the ghosts than to deal with them."

Victor stared at Lindsey. "But you can't ignore them because your gift is stronger."

"It's like they know I can see them? Or maybe it's just that I'm not good at hiding the fact that I can. I don't know. Until now, I've always tried to ignore ghosts, but it never worked well."

"And you've stopped trying to do that?"

Lindsey looked at Jerome and then Marcel. "I don't have the luxury to do that anymore. Besides, this gift is a part of me. Maybe I shouldn't be ignoring it."

Victor sipped on his coffee. "I'll be happy to teach you and Will how to deal with this gift." His gaze stopped on Marcel, who was ready to jump on the table and start screaming that Victor was here for him, dammit.

He understood how shocked Will had been to find out he could see ghosts, though, and he wanted Will to have the possibility of learning how to deal with it. From the way Lindsey made it sound, it wasn't easy.

"And to help you as much as I can," Victor continued.

"*Can* you help me?" Marcel asked.

Victor put down his cup of coffee. "I've seen this kind of thing a few times. Not often, mind you, and I could be wrong about what's causing this, so I have a few questions I'd like you to answer."

Marcel stopped pacing the length of the room and faced Victor from the other side of the table. He was standing by Jerome, and even though his brother couldn't see him, Marcel knew he was there to support him. It only helped a tiny bit, but it was something.

"I'll answer any question you might have that I can. I don't remember what happened to me, though."

Victor nodded. "Not surprising."

"I'll answer anything I can."

Victor bit on his lower lip and looked around. "I'm assuming these people are close to you?"

"The closest they could be. Jerome is my brother and Lindsey's boyfriend, and I grew up with Will."

Lindsey was leaning close to Jerome, whispering what Marcel was saying to him so he could stay in the loop. It had to be hard for him to be the only one unable to see and hear Marcel. Marcel desperately wished he could talk to his brother, but this would have to do for now.

Victor looked relieved. "If Jerome is your brother, you probably share the same gift."

"We're not psychic," Marcel said with a frown.

"I didn't expect you to be. But I do think you're some kind of shifter."

Marcel stared. Humans weren't usually aware of shifters. Marcel supposed things were different for psychics, since they weren't like other humans. "We are," he confirmed. "Dragon shifters."

"That explains a lot. You're a powerful shifter, which means you have a lot of life energy to use."

None of this made sense. "I don't know what you're talking about. This had to be an accident. I'm probably somewhere in a hospital." That was the only thing Marcel had been able to come up with to explain what was going on.

There were holes in that reasoning. The hospital would have called his family.

Marcel and Jerome's mother was going to kill them when she found out about this and that they didn't tell her right away.

Victor's expression turned sad. "I don't think you are. It's a possibility, but again, I've seen this several times before.

You may be in a coma in a hospital, but I suspect that what's happening here is that someone is keeping you in a coma to use your life energy."

Will had been happy when Victor had arrived. He'd thought they'd get answers, but so far, everything was still as confusing as it had been before.

"What does that mean?" he asked before he could stop himself.

Victor didn't seem angry. "Some people do that, usually humans. It could be psychics, or maybe mages or witches. There's no way to know, unfortunately."

"You're going to have to give us more details, because I have no idea what you're saying."

Victor nodded. "I could be wrong. I'm sure there are other occasions in which a shifter ends up out of his body, but the few times I've stumbled onto something like this, that was what was happening. Shifters, especially predators, have a lot of life energy. They need it to be able to shift, and of course, they are two beings inside of one person. That's twice the life energy a human would have, and with dragons, it's even more energy. Some people want to use that energy, and I think they got their hands on Marcel."

Will swallowed. That didn't sound good. "What are they doing with it?"

"Your guess is as good as mine. Usually, it's nothing good, which is one more reason for us to stop them."

"So you're staying and helping us?" Jerome intervened.

Victor nodded. "For more than one reason. I'd like to help Lindsey and Will with their gift, as well as getting Marcel back to his body and finding out what's going on. If someone is using the life energy of a dragon shifter, it means that whatever they're doing is a problem, and a big one. People who steal life energy aren't the kind of people you want as your friend."

That meant that whatever they were doing with Marcel's energy wasn't good.

Will sighed. His life had been so easy when it was just him and Jerome. After Lindsey had barged into it, it had become complicated, and Will wished it hadn't. He didn't begrudge Lindsey for any of this, though. Without him, they wouldn't have known to call Victor, and that meant they wouldn't have been able to help Marcel.

Will had never been part of the supernatural world. He'd been at the fringe of it since he was friends with Marcel and Jerome, but he wasn't *in* it. He wasn't sure how much that had changed now that he knew he was a psychic, but he was afraid to ask. He was also afraid of what the supernatural world wanted from Marcel. Victor seemed to believe it wasn't good, and Will agreed. Whoever was ready to steal life energy from someone couldn't be up to anything that wouldn't end in pain.

Jerome huffed. "My life wasn't this complicated before."

Lindsey glared at him. "You mean before you met me?"

Will prayed they wouldn't start bickering. Now wasn't the moment for them to fight and make up. Thankfully, Jerome snatched Lindsey behind the neck and pulled him close for a kiss that made Will look away. His gaze crossed with Marcel's, and they smiled at each other. They'd both been traumatized by Jerome and Lindsey's inability to keep their hands off each other, and it created a sort of kinship between them.

Victor cleared his throat. That was when Will remembered that not everyone was okay with two men being together. He eyed Victor, wary of the man's reaction, but Victor was smiling. "I think I'm going to have fun here," he said.

Will didn't know about fun, but this certainly was going to be complicated.

Victor turned his attention to Will. "So, Will, I already know a lot about Lindsey from the online forum we met on. What about you?"

Will blinked. "What about me?"

"The only thing I know about you is that you never saw ghosts until recently, or at least, that you don't believe you did."

"I talked to my parents this morning, and my great-grandmother was a psychic, or at least, that's what my father says. That's really all I know."

"Well, I can't tell how strong your gift is, but we'll find out when you start training."

Victor had said something about training both Lindsey and Will earlier, but Will hadn't really stopped to think about it. "I don't know if I want to be trained. I've seen how annoyed Lindsey was at some ghosts, and I've heard his horror stories. I don't know if I can deal with that."

Victor didn't look angry, but Will wasn't surprised he wasn't giving up. "You certainly can choose to ignore your gift, but what will happen when ghosts start realizing you can see them? You need to be able to push them away and close your mind to them, and ignore them. The only way to obtain that is through training."

"Maybe my gift won't be strong enough to warrant training." Because Will didn't feel he could deal with more things on his plate.

"How about this? I want to focus on Marcel first, and I might need your and Lindsey's help. I can try to find out how strong your gift is as we do that, and once all of this is over, we'll talk again."

"How long is the training going to take?"

"That's impossible to say. It depends on how quickly you take to it."

"You're not from here, though, right?"

"I'm not. That's one of the reasons it took me a few days to arrive. But I wouldn't have a problem relocating to town."

"You'd relocate just for us?"

The smile Victor gave him was a bit sad. "Not just for you. I've been thinking about doing it for a while now, and this is the perfect excuse. Besides, I'm looking forward to working with you and Lindsey."

"Have you ever taught anyone this stuff?" Lindsey asked.

"Once."

When it was obvious he wouldn't elaborate, Lindsey nodded and changed the topic of conversation. "What about Marcel? Have you already helped someone in his situation?"

Victor hesitated. "Not me, but my teacher. I was too inexperienced."

Will didn't understand how one could be inexperienced talking to ghosts, but considering he hadn't known he could do it until today, he didn't feel it was his place to say anything about it.

He was glad they'd met Victor. There was no way to know what would happen next, but they were all working to help Marcel, and Will believed they'd manage to do it.

They had to.

CHAPTER THREE

Marcel had followed Will last night. There was no way he was going home, not when there was a chance he'd see his brother and Lindsey going at it again. Jerome had promised they'd keep that kind of activity to the bedroom, but Marcel didn't believe they could. They were still in the first phase of their relationship, and they couldn't keep their hands off each other. Besides, it was their home. They shouldn't have to be careful about what they did or didn't do to accommodate Marcel.

Will hadn't minded when Marcel asked him if he could go with him. Marcel supposed he didn't really need a place to stay. He could stick around the office and wait for everyone to come back the next day. He'd discovered that he didn't really sleep, even when he tried to. He didn't need food, either, or the bathroom. The office would have been enough for him, but it would have also been lonely. Going home with Will, Marcel had been able to spend the evening in his company, and it helped.

But now, as he was stretched out on the couch staring at the ceiling, he wondered what happened when he slept. It wasn't really sleep, not the way he slept when he was human. It was almost as if he just lost periods of time, and he didn't know what happened when he did. Did he stay here, on Will's couch? Did he end up somewhere else, maybe where his body was? If that was the case, could he make it happen on purpose and try to see where his body was?

Marcel had a lot of questions, and he wanted to ask Victor

all of them.

Victor had spent the entire previous day with Marcel, along with Will and Lindsey. He'd asked a lot of questions about what Marcel had been up to in his last memories, and while it had been frustrating, Marcel had repeated the entire story. He'd thought that once he was done, Victor would tell him how to fix things, but instead, he'd gotten to his feet and had declared he needed to get to his hotel room. Marcel had wanted to scream, but he'd kept himself under control. He had no idea what was happening, while Victor was the one of them who knew the most about it. Whatever he'd needed to do in his hotel room, it had to be important.

A sound coming from the hallway made Marcel sit up. He didn't know what time it was, but considering the light that had started appearing at the window, it was probably almost time for Will to get up.

Sure enough, Will appeared a few moments later, rubbing his face with both his hands. He was only wearing boxers, and Marcel couldn't look away.

He'd always considered Will another brother. The two of them and Jerome had grown up together, and while they'd drifted slightly apart over the years, they were still friends. That was all Will had been to Marcel until now, and Marcel wondered if things would have been different if they'd kept in closer touch.

Because Will wasn't his brother. He was a man, and he was really fucking sexy. How could Marcel not have realized that sooner?

He'd seen Will half-naked plenty of times, but that had always been when they were kids and teenagers. It hadn't happened since then, and Marcel had been missing out on that. The fact that he was staring at Will's naked chest made him feel like a creep, but he couldn't help but take in the long muscles, slightly hairy chest, and dark trail that led down into his boxers. Where Marcel had a bit of a stomach and was broad-shouldered, Will was tall and slim and muscled.

Marcel wanted to grab him, pull him onto the couch, and kiss him, but even if Will wouldn't have a problem with that, Marcel couldn't touch him. It didn't matter that his fingers tingled with the need to do just that.

Will dropped his hands, saw Marcel, and screamed.

Marcel had been getting to his feet, but now, he fell back against the couch, raising both his hands. Will's cat had been sleeping on the windowsill, and she launched herself off and disappeared down the hallway, almost colliding with Will's legs.

Will stopped screaming almost instantly, but his eyes were still wide, and he pressed a hand against his chest. "I forgot you were there," he said.

"Sorry. I didn't mean to scare you."

Will shook his head. "It's not your fault. I'm just not used to having people sleep on my couch."

"I can leave if you want me to." Marcel got up again. It was obvious Will wasn't used to sharing his living space, period. Marcel doubted he would have come into the living room only wearing boxer shorts otherwise.

Will looked down at his body, and his cheeks and chest flushed. "Sorry about this. I'll just grab a t-shirt."

He disappeared back into the hallway before Marcel could tell him he didn't mind. Maybe it was better this way. Marcel didn't want to make a mess out of a situation that was already messy enough as it was. Adding a crush on Will to it didn't feel like the best thing to do, but he realized he wouldn't be able to stop himself from crushing on Will if that was what happened. What he *could* do was not do anything about it, no matter how much he wanted to.

Will reappeared only moments later, wearing a t-shirt and a pair of loose shorts. Marcel regretted not being able to look at his body, but Will appeared more comfortable now, and that was all that mattered.

"Jerome said you didn't eat with them yesterday," Will said as he started coffee.

"That's because I don't think I'd be able to eat. I'm not hungry, anyway."

Will nodded. "I didn't think you could. I mean, you're a ghost."

"Hopefully, that's not what I am, but yeah." Because if Marcel truly was a ghost, it meant he was dead.

He didn't want to be dead.

"What I meant is that considering you can't touch anything, it makes sense that you can't eat, either."

"Feel free to eat breakfast. I'm happy sitting with you and talking."

Will grinned. "Happier than you were yesterday morning?"

A flash of what he'd seen yesterday morning passed through Marcel's mind, and he grimaced. "Why did you have to remind me of that?" he whined.

"I've walked in on them several times. It's only fair I share the misery."

Marcel laughed. He might be complaining about Jerome and Lindsey, but he was happy for his brother. "They really love each other, don't they?" he asked as Will settled at the table with a loaf of bread and peanut butter and jelly.

"They do. I know it's weird because they always snap at each other, but they've been like that since they met. Jerome wasn't the nicest person when Lindsey first walked into our office, but he redeemed himself."

Marcel wrinkled his nose. "Let me guess. He wasn't happy Lindsey is human."

"You know how he is with humans."

"Yet you're in his life and proof that humans can be nice

people."

Will shrugged. "But I've known him since we were kids. I've been his best friend for just as long. Knowing what he went through with some humans, I can understand why he was wary. The important thing is that he gave Lindsey a chance and that they're together now."

The coffee machine signaled that it was done brewing, and Will got back to his feet. Marcel watched him move, wishing he could help. He felt like a dick, not getting breakfast ready, or at least starting the coffee. "Sorry about not starting coffee for you," he said.

"I didn't expect you to. You can't touch the machine."

"I can't, and I hate all of this. I just want my body back."

Will reached over the table, but he couldn't touch Marcel's arm, not even for comfort. He took his hand back, and Marcel really wished he could feel him.

"I can only imagine how hard this is, but I promise we'll do everything we can to get you back to your body. You heard Victor. This isn't over by any means. We have him on our side now, and he's going to help." Will sounded more confident than Marcel felt.

"I know." And Marcel didn't think Will and the others were lying. They'd truly do everything they could to help.

But would it be enough?

Will was surprised how much he enjoyed having Marcel around his apartment. He'd never shared it with anyone but his cat, and while it was odd, it also felt good. Besides, he was happy to be able to give this to Marcel. It wasn't a lot, but hopefully, it was a bit of comfort.

He went back to his bedroom to get dressed and found Cleo on his bed. "There you are. I was wondering where you were at," he said, rubbing the soft skin on top of her head.

Usually she spent the evening with him, but he hadn't seen her anywhere last night. He suspected it had to do with Marcel, and he hoped Cleo would get used to having him around. Maybe she'd be of some comfort to Marcel, too.

"He's a good person," he promised the Sphinx cat. "You just have to get to know him."

She raised her nose as if that wasn't good enough for her. She was a spoiled brat, and it was entirely Will's fault.

With a chuckle and one last cuddle, he got to his feet and headed to the bathroom. He needed to get dressed so he and Marcel could head to the office. Wasting time in his apartment talking to his cat wouldn't help Marcel get back to his body, and the sooner that happened, the better it would be.

It hurt him to see how lost and angry Marcel was. Will wanted to do everything he could to help him, but he wasn't sure there *was* anything he could do. Victor had sounded hopeful yesterday, which Will supposed made sense since he knew what was happening, but Will was still lost. He had a hard time believing he'd been a psychic this entire time and hadn't realized it. He was a PI, for fuck's sake. He should have noticed this a long time ago. Of course, if he had, he doubted Jerome and Lindsey would have met, so maybe it wasn't a bad thing.

It still made him uneasy. Was there anything else about himself that he didn't know? Any gift he could use to help Marcel?

Marcel was on the couch again when Will went back to the living room. Will had turned on the TV for him before going to get ready, but Marcel didn't seem interested in the news. He was staring at the ceiling, but he looked at Will when he heard him and smiled.

"Ready to go when you are," Will said.

"Please."

"You were bored?"

Marcel sighed. "It has nothing to do with you. I just can't touch anything, not even the remote control. It's incredibly frustrating to need someone to do everything for me."

"I can understand that, but unfortunately, you don't have a choice. I want you to know I'll help you anytime you need me, for whatever you need."

They headed out. Will kept his mouth shut until they reached the car, since he didn't want his neighbors to think he was nuts. He supposed a lot of people talk to themselves even when they couldn't see ghosts, but still.

There was nothing much he could do for Marcel, but he could distract him, so, as soon as they were in the car, he said, "Tell me about York."

Will was curious about the kind of guys Marcel dated, and a bit jealous. It didn't make sense, since he and Marcel had only ever been friends, but he couldn't deny he was attracted to Marcel.

"What do you want to know?" Marcel asked as he tried to put on his seatbelt and gave up. He'd tried last night, too.

"Whatever you want to tell me. What kind of guy is he? You said he was young, and you described him, but that's all I know about him."

Marcel shrugged and looked out the window. "There's nothing much to say. He's a nice guy. I'd barely gotten to know him before this happened, to be honest."

"Do you think you'll want to see him again once this is over?"

"I don't know. None of this is his fault, but I don't think I can date him. I feel like spending time with him would be too much of a reminder of what's happening to me."

Clearly, Marcel wasn't in the mood to talk about York. That was fine with Will, who decided to choose another topic of conversation. "I know you can't exactly pick up the phone and call, but do you think we should tell your parents what's happening?"

Marcel grimaced. "Probably. You know my mother. She's going to kill us when she finds out about this."

And she would. Corinne was a force to be reckoned with. That was probably one of the reasons Marcel didn't want to tell her to begin with.

"I just don't want to scare her," Marcel continued. "I know she'll try to help, and I'm starting to wonder if maybe we might need her and the clan's help, but she's going to freak out."

"I wouldn't blame her. You're her son, and you're in trouble."

"And I get that. I already have enough to deal with, though. I don't know if I can deal with her and the clan, too."

"You know her better than I do, so I'll follow your lead. We all will."

Marcel snorted. "You know her as well as I do. You spent your childhood with her."

"True, but she's not my mother."

"You think I should call her."

"Well, since she probably won't be able to see you, I think your brother should."

Marcel barked out a laugh. "Right. I won't have to tell her because I can't."

"She'll be unable to talk to you, but I think she should know. I'd want my parents to know if something like this happened to me, and I'd want to know if someone I care about was in your situation."

Marcel groaned. "That means I need to call Leo, too."

"That's your best friend?" Will asked, even though he was pretty sure he was right.

"He is. He's going to be pissed, too."

"What happened to you isn't your fault."

"Not for that. He's going to be pissed I didn't have Jerome

or someone else call him the second they could. He's probably frantic right now. Hell, I'd be surprised if he hasn't called Mom and Dad yet. It's a miracle they didn't call Jerome yesterday."

Will agreed it was. If they knew something was happening, they'd probably have been in the office yesterday, demanding answers and wanting to know where Marcel was.

Brent, Marcel's father, had always been more laid-back than his wife. Maybe it was because he was human, while Marcel's mother was a dragon shifter. The two of them now lived with a dragon clan, but when Marcel and Jerome were young, they'd lived in the house next to Will's. That was how the three of them had become friends.

As soon as Marcel's parents knew what was happening, they'd pull the clan into it, and Will could understand why Marcel didn't want that to happen. An entire dragon clan wasn't easy to control, especially when one of theirs was in trouble.

"I'll ask Jerome to make the calls once we're at the office," Marcel said.

He didn't sound happy about that, but Will hoped that having the dragons on their side meant they'd find a way to help Marcel. It was great to have Victor, and hopefully, he'd be able to fix this, but it would be good to have the backup, too.

"Everything will be fine," he promised.

"Don't you know my mother?"

Will laughed. "I do, just like you know mine. Yes, she's going to freak out and want to go out there right away to help, but once the first moment of panic passes, it'll be good to have her with us. She's a rock in this kind of situation."

She always had been. When Jerome had broken his wing while flying in his dragon form, his father had panicked and had wanted to find a vet, while Jerome's mother had calmly decided to contact the nearby dragon clan to ask if they had a healer. When Marcel had disappeared from his bedroom one night when they were teenagers, Brent had wanted to call the police, while Corinne had called Will to ask him if he'd seen Marcel.

He had. Marcel had been in his bedroom, angry with his parents after a fight they'd had.

It would be good to have Corinne and Brent's help. Besides, they needed all the help they could find.

Victor was already at the office when they, which meant Marcel might finally be able to go back to his body. He peeked at Will, wondering how the other man felt. Finding out he was a psychic had taken him for a loop, and that couldn't be easy. Of course, being suddenly dead—or not—wasn't easy, either.

Marcel thought that the worst part of this was not knowing what was happening to him. He wanted to know if he was dead so he could start making his peace with it if that was the case. Victor had said he wasn't, and he wanted to believe it, but could he? He didn't know Victor. Victor might be the only one with experience in this kind of situation, and he might have seen this a few times already, but Marcel was afraid to believe him only to be disappointed in the end.

No, the best way for him to go about this would be to go back to his body. Then he could believe he was alive.

Since the office was still closed, Victor had been waiting out front. He didn't seem to mind, and he smiled when he noticed Will and Marcel walking toward him. They'd parked behind the office, but they walked around the building since Victor was there.

"Good morning," Victor said with a small wave.

"You could have called me," Will answered as he took out his keys. "We would have come sooner."

"I didn't mind waiting."

He'd had his face buried in his phone before, but now, the phone was nowhere to be seen. Marcel looked him up and down, wondering if this really was the guy who would help him. He was dressed like yesterday, in dark jeans and a dark button-up shirt, with that tattoo peeking from the collar. His dark hair was styled away from his face, and the silver rings on his fingers glinted in the sunlight. He looked good, but not as good as Will, in Marcel's opinion.

Will let both of them in and closed the front door. He looked at them, then gestured toward the break room. "Lindsey and Jerome will come in through the back door. I don't know if you're ready to start, Victor, but we should probably wait for them."

"I wouldn't mind another cup of coffee," Victor said.

Marcel groaned. "I want coffee, too."

"I'll get it for you as soon as you're back in your body," Will promised.

Marcel was pretty sure he couldn't feel pain or anything else, really. He didn't feel hunger or thirst. He didn't feel sleepy, either. But hearing Will making promises that they'd get coffee together once everything was back to normal made something churn in his stomach.

What had Will meant? Would it be coffee here in the break room? Or would it be more like a date, where they'd go to a coffee shop? Marcel was surprised at how much he wanted the second option to be what Will was talking about, even though it also made him nervous.

He'd met York in a coffee shop.

It seemed like that was where everything started. Marcel didn't want to blame York, especially since he didn't know if the man had anything to do with what happened to him, but he couldn't help but wonder.

Marcel had noticed York when he'd walked into the coffee

shop, but he hadn't given him much thought. It was York who'd come to him, asking to sit with him at the table and introducing himself. Marcel had been the one to ask him out, but York had taken the first step toward Marcel. Did that mean something? If it did, *what* did it mean?

Marcel doubted he'd get answers anytime soon. He'd have to find York, and he didn't think he would. He was starting to believe that York had something to do with what was happening to him, even though he didn't want to. The man had been sweet, but Marcel couldn't deny something was wrong.

Something was *very* wrong, considering he wasn't in his body.

Luckily, Lindsey and Jerome arrived only ten minutes later. Lindsey looked sleepy, but Jerome was frowning. It was an expression Marcel had often seen on his brother, and he wished he weren't the reason Jerome felt this way today.

"When are we starting?" he asked as he walked into the break room.

"Good morning to you, too," Will drawled.

Jerome barely looked at him. "Good morning. So? When are we starting?" he asked Victor.

Victor had been sipping on his coffee, but he didn't look angry at Jerome's harsh tone. "As soon as you want. Maybe it would be better if you went to work. Will and Lindsey will be here because I want them to watch since they need to learn, but you don't have to."

Jerome crossed his arms over his chest, making his muscles bunch under his t-shirt. "I'm not going anywhere."

He'd clearly been trying to intimidate Victor, but it didn't look like it worked. Victor kept the smile on his face and patiently nodded as if dealing with a child. "All right. It shouldn't be a problem. I just thought that considering the three of you here are PIs and we're in your office, you had things to do."

"I'll get back to work once I know my brother is safe," Jerome said.

"Completely understandable," Victor agreed.

He turned his attention to Lindsey and Will. "As I was saying, I'd like both of you to be here. I think that watching this could teach you a lot."

His words made Marcel nervous. What was he going to do that he could teach Lindsey and Will about it? Would it hurt? Marcel was more than a little nervous, but he wasn't backing down. He couldn't afford to.

"Neither of us is going anywhere," Will told Victor.

Marcel knew everyone here cared about him, but hearing it touched him. That went especially for Will and Lindsey. Will had always been Jerome's best friend more than Marcel's. As for Lindsey, Marcel didn't know him. It would have been logical for him to leave, but instead, here he was. It wasn't just that he was eager to learn, either. He seemed truly worried, even though he barely knew Marcel.

"Why don't you sit on the couch?" Victor asked as he gestured at it.

"Do you think it'll change anything?" Marcel asked as he moved to obey.

"I doubt it, but at least you'll be more comfortable."

"I'm a ghost. I'm never uncomfortable."

Victor's smile was indulgent. "You might feel like that, but even though you're not in your body, you're still human. It's normal for you to associate the couch with being more comfortable than a chair."

Marcel supposed it made sense. Even if it hadn't, he would have obeyed. Victor was the only one who knew what he was doing, or at least, Marcel hoped he did.

Marcel sat. It was odd to have everyone stare at him, but he'd deal if it meant getting back to his body.

"Please close your eyes," Victor said. He moved closer,

taking his chair and setting it in front of Marcel.

Marcel closed his eyes, but he could tell that Victor had sat in the chair. His voice was even closer now.

"I want you to relax. I realize it might not be easy considering the stress you've been dealing with, but it's important."

Marcel sucked in a breath. He'd do everything Victor wanted him to do, even if he asked him to wear a tutu and dance around the office.

"Think of your physical body," Victor continued.

His voice was softer now, gentler, and it lulled Marcel into what would have been sleep if he'd been in his body. As it was, it just helped him relax, and he couldn't say he minded. Victor's voice was soothing, and it came at a moment Marcel needed that.

"Think of how being in your body feels."

That was even weirder. Marcel had never thought about what being in his body felt like. He hoped it wouldn't ruin everything if he got it wrong.

He did his best, but nothing happened. He didn't know how long he stayed there, sitting with his eyes closed, but what Victor said with his gentle voice didn't matter. It wasn't doing anything, and Marcel had enough.

He was about to tell Victor it was time to stop, but before he could, something happened. He felt like he'd moved, even though he was sure he hadn't. The world twisted around him, which was odd, to say the least, since he couldn't see anything. When he opened his eyes, he wasn't in the break room anymore.

Will knew the instant something happened to Marcel. Marcel's back went ramrod straight, and he sucked in a sudden breath. Will moved to go to him and help him if he was in distress, but Victor raised a hand to stop him. Will wanted to protest, but Victor was the only one who knew what he was doing. He couldn't afford to get this wrong, especially when this might be the only way to help Marcel.

Will stopped moving, but he hovered close to Marcel, ready to help if he needed him.

"Can you still hear me?" Victor asked.

"Am I allowed to speak now?" Marcel answered.

Victor chuckled. "I never said you weren't allowed to speak. But yes, I'd like you to tell me where you are."

Will waited, holding his breath.

"I don't know," Marcel said.

Will started breathing again. It had been too much to hope they could solve this right away. It was already a lot that Marcel had been able to find his body. Will should have known better than to hope for more today.

"So you're not in a place you've ever been in?" Victor pushed.

Will had to remember it wasn't over. None of them expected any of this to be easy. Whoever had gotten their hands on Marcel had to know there was a possibility he might find his body. That meant they kept him hidden and that it probably would be harder to find him.

"I'm on my back. I can feel someone is holding my hand, but I can't open my eyes," Marcel said.

"Can you try again?" Victor asked. "It doesn't matter if you can't, but I'd like you to try."

There was a moment of silence before Marcel shook his head. "Nothing. I'm sorry."

"That's fine," Victor reassured him. "How about the person holding your hand? Can you tell who it is?"

"Not without opening my eyes."

"Tell me about the hand, then. Is it a woman's hand? A man's?"

"I think it's a guy." Marcel paused, then swore. "Dammit.

I can't tell anything else."

"That's okay," Victor said. "If there's nothing else you can gather from your body, you can come back to us."

Will stared at Marcel. Marcel blinked, and as soon as his eyes were open, Will reached for him. He stopped just in time, and it was awkward to hover his hand over Marcel's shoulder instead of clasping it. He wanted to comfort Marcel, but how could he when he couldn't touch the man?

"You did good," Victor said once Marcel was looking at him.

"How can you say that? I didn't learn anything. I don't know what happened to me or where my body is. I don't even know who that man holding my hand is."

"You can't expect to be able to do this right away. It's going to take you a while to go back to your body and use it. There's a reason you're in this position, Marcel. Someone made sure you wouldn't be able to get out of this easily, if at all. You're lucky you know a psychic who knew to call me. Think about what would have happened if you hadn't."

Marcel's shoulders slumped. "I'd be completely lost. I get what you're saying, but this is frustrating."

Victor smiled gently. "I understand. I wish I could do more for you, but at the moment, this is a great result. I'm sure you're tired now."

Marcel nodded, looking grumpy. "I feel like I've run a marathon instead of just sitting here on the couch."

"That's normal. Most people aren't used to using their minds the way you just did. It's like a muscle. You need to train it before being able to use it more than you did today."

"What can I do to train it?"

"You can repeat what you just did. Find a comfortable place, close your eyes, and focus on your body. It's going to tire you a lot, especially in the beginning. You need to push through that and continue doing it. Eventually, you'll be able to control your body more. You'll be able to open your eyes and look at what's around you, and maybe even to move more."

"Can't I just stay in it?"

"Unfortunately, that's not how it works. I need to find out what the psychic or whoever has you did to you and reverse it. Until that happens, you'll be like a visitor in your body."

Will's heart ached for Marcel. He wanted to help him, but how could he? All of them were already doing everything they could, including Victor.

Jerome looked even grumpier than Marcel. Lindsey had stood next to him the entire time, whispering what was happening to his brother. "When will he try again?" he asked.

"Not for a few hours, at least," Victor said. "This is something that takes a lot out of the spirit."

"We should get to work, then."

"Actually, I'd like to talk to Lindsey and Will."

Jerome huffed. "Of course you would. Well, *I'm* going to work, since I'm useless."

Will understood how he felt. Marcel was his brother, and Jerome wanted to protect him. He had in every other situation, but in this case, there was nothing he could do. He was even less useful than Will and Lindsey, and they were useless, too, which was saying something.

"What do you need us to do?" Lindsey asked once Jerome left.

Will kept an eye on Marcel, who looked like he was sleeping. His eyes were closed, and he was still sitting on the couch. Marcel had told him he didn't sleep, though, so he was probably just resting.

"Nothing for today." Victor got up and moved his chair back to the table. "I just want to go over what psychics can or can't do, and maybe more importantly, what they should or shouldn't do. I realize you want to start training right away so you can help Marcel, but you need to know some things first."

Will wasn't surprised, even though he did want to start helping in any way he could.

"We're listening," he said.

Victor spread both his hands on the table and stared at them for a moment. There were scars on his long fingers that Will wanted to ask about, but he knew better than to be that rude.

"There are no rules when it comes to being a psychic, so you'll have to be the one to decide what you will or will not do. Most people just help the dead cross over if they can or soothe their families. Others take advantage of the dead and manipulate them."

Will grimaced. "That's not something I want to do."

"I agree," Lindsey intervened. "I just want to be able to block the dead out when I need to. You don't know how many jobs I lost because they were trying to get my attention and made a mess when I didn't give it to them. Is there a way to do that?"

Victor looked relieved. "There is, and I'll teach you. I'll also teach you how to close your mind so you don't see them for a short length of time and to call them and have them answer your questions."

Will hadn't expected to be able to do all those things, but then, he hadn't had a lot of time to think about what he could do as a psychic. But Lindsey looked excited, and Will was starting to feel the same. He hadn't known he had this gift, and he didn't know what to do with it, but that was why he was here. He wanted to learn and to use his gift for good. The first thing would be to help Marcel, but once that was done, Will would be able to use his gift to help on the cases he and Jerome worked on.

He leaned forward, eager to listen to what Victor had to

say. He didn't know how long Victor would stay, although the man had said he'd be willing to relocate. In the meantime, Will would take advantage of every moment Victor was willing to teach him and Lindsey how to do this.

Chapter Four

Marcel tried to make it work for hours after Victor talked him through the first time. There was nothing different, no matter how many times he tried, and by the end of the day, he was exhausted. The only thing he wanted to do was go to sleep, but he wasn't even sure he could. Besides, they had something to do, and he wasn't looking forward to it.

They were visiting his parents tonight.

"We'll try again tomorrow," Victor promised.

Strangely, Marcel trusted him. He'd only known Victor a couple days, but they'd worked together for hours, and he liked the guy. He wasn't happy about how they'd met or why they were spending time together, but it felt like Victor could become a friend, and Marcel wanted to see if that was the case. Besides, Victor was also helping Lindsey and Will, so he wasn't going anywhere anytime soon.

"I'll hold you to that," Marcel said.

Victor's smile was gentle. "I can only imagine how frustrating and terrifying this is for you. Considering the situation, I think you're doing great. I know you wish we could do things faster, and so do I, but as far as I know, this is the only way for us to find out where you are."

He explained a bit about what they'd need to do once they did find Marcel's body, but Marcel didn't understand much. "And you need to know where my body is because the only way to get me back into it is to know what that psychic did to me," he said, hoping he'd gotten it right.

Victor nodded. "It's obvious they worked with a mage or a

witch. There are several ways to separate a spirit from its body, and we need to know how they did it for you. But I don't want you to push yourself, because it wouldn't help. Continue trying to find out where your body is, but not if you get a headache or if you're too tired. You don't want to cause damage to your body."

Marcel hadn't known that was a possibility, but he'd heed Victor's warning. Victor was the only one of them who knew what he was doing, after all.

"Ready?" Lindsey asked, interrupting the conversation between Victor and Marcel.

Victor got to his feet. "I'll head to my hotel room. You have plans tonight?"

Marcel grimaced. "We need to tell my parents what's happening."

"And you're not looking forward to it."

"They'll both freak out, and knowing my mother, she'll try pulling in the clan."

Victor's expression changed. "You're part of a dragon clan, then?"

"My parents are. They weren't always, but once Jerome and I left the house, they moved. My mother is a dragon, but my father is human. That doesn't mean he's any less fierce than she is when it comes to protecting their kids, though. They're going to freak out, and I don't know how I'll deal with it."

Will repeated Marcel's words to the others. It was bothersome for everyone, but necessary.

"You won't," Jerome grumped as he walked in, too. "*I'll* have to deal with them, since they can't see you. I'll remember this when Christmas comes and I have to pick your gifts."

"It's not my fault I'm a spirit," Marcel argued. It felt good to tease and bicker with his brother, almost like everything was back to normal.

"Feel free to give them my number," Victor said. "I'll answer any questions they might have. And who knows, maybe the clan's help will make it easier to find your body. Having you go to it isn't the only way to do that, after all."

Marcel hadn't thought of that. After Victor had explained what Marcel should do, Marcel had focused on that. But his brother, Lindsey, and Will were private investigators. Who better than them to find Marcel's body? That was something they'd have to talk about, but not right now.

Victor left, and Jerome locked up the office. Will hovered close to Marcel as if he expected Marcel to faint or something like that, which puzzled Marcel a bit. "I'm fine," he promised.

"I'm not sure about that. You look tired."

"I am, but I promise I'm okay. I'm not looking forward to seeing my parents, though."

"We'll all be there for you."

Marcel frowned. "Are you coming, too?"

"I am, and so is Lindsey."

"I didn't expect that. I didn't think Lindsey would want to meet my parents for the first time in this kind of situation."

Will shrugged. "It's not like I'm looking forward to seeing them considering everything, but we're going to work together to get you back to your body. We might as well do this."

Marcel supposed he was right.

He decided to ride with Will, just in case Jerome and Lindsey decided to stop for a quickie somewhere. Marcel didn't think they would, but he enjoyed teasing them about it. Anything rather than think about what he'd walk into once he reached his parents' house.

The drive was silent, and Marcel took the opportunity to rest, but it wasn't easy. He couldn't stop thinking about what was happening to him, and not just about the basics like where his body was and who was hurting him. How could he be in this car when he couldn't touch stuff? Why wasn't he passing through the seat? None of it made sense, and he doubted anyone could give him these answers except maybe Victor, but he had more important things to focus on.

Marcel closed his eyes and leaned his head back against the seat, emptying his mind. He was tempted to try to find his body again, but he remembered what Victor had said about not doing it if he was too tired. It might do more harm than good, and that was the last thing Marcel wanted.

Jerome had called their parents, so they knew they were coming. As soon as Jerome and Will parked in front of the house, the door flew open, and Marcel saw his mother standing there. His chest squeezed. Right now, he wanted nothing more than to run to her and throw himself into her arms. He might be a full-grown adult, but his mother still gave the best hugs, and he desperately needed one. Instead, he had to watch as she hugged Jerome, Will, and even Lindsey, who looked bewildered but happy.

"Where's Marcel?" she asked, looking around their little group. "When you said you were coming, I thought he'd be with you."

"I need to talk to you and Dad about him," Jerome said.

She looked wary, but she led them into the kitchen. Marcel took a deep breath, and even though he wasn't sure he needed to do that as a spirit, the familiarity helped soothe him.

"Do I need to call Elijah?" Marcel's mom asked.

That got the attention of Marcel's father, who looked up from his crosswords book with a frown. "Why would you need to call the alpha?" he asked.

Lindsey was looking around with interest, and he'd perked up at those words.

Marcel knew he was curious and that he'd never met shifters before Jerome, so he moved closer. "The clan doesn't live together like some packs do, but they do live close to each other. Everyone on the street belongs to the clan. Hell, everyone in this neighborhood does. The alpha's house is only a few houses away."

"This is fascinating," Lindsey murmured.

"I'm sure Jerome will tell you everything you might want to know later," Marcel said.

Lindsey's expression hardened again. "We're here for you, not for my amusement."

"Maybe, but it's your first time meeting your in-laws. I understand this is weird for you."

Lindsey paled. "I almost forgot they're my in-laws."

Marcel laughed and turned to their little group. Both his parents were staring at Lindsey as if not quite understanding what he was doing. It made sense since it looked like he was talking to himself.

"Lindsey is a psychic," Jerome explained. "And my boyfriend. Mom, Dad, this is Lindsey, my boyfriend. Lindsey, these are my parents, Corinne and Brent."

Lindsey rubbed his hands on his jeans and went to say hello. Marcel's parents were happy to meet him but still worried, so Marcel was glad the introduction was kept short. His mother offered everyone a drink, but she kept looking around as if searching for Marcel.

Once everyone had declined her offer for a drink, she blurted out, "Where's Marcel?"

Jerome sighed. "We're here because something's happened to him."

Both their parents paled so much that Marcel was worried. "He's alive," Will hurried to add. "But right now, his spirit isn't in his body. We don't know what happened to him exactly, but we'll find out, and we'll save him. In the meantime, he's hanging around us in his spirit form."

"Can you explain all this again?" Marcel's father asked.

This time, it was Lindsey who explained. He made sure

both of Marcel's parents were following and gave them all the details they wanted. When they asked where Marcel was, Lindsey pointed at him. Even though they couldn't see him, they still came closer, hovering by Marcel and staring at him. He wanted to hug them, but the only thing he could do was stand there and stare. He couldn't wait for all of this to be over.

The problem was that there was no way for him to be sure that once it was, he'd be alive.

Will hung back, letting the family deal with each other. He cared about everyone involved, and it hurt to see the pain on Corinne and Brent's faces. He wanted to help, but there wasn't anything he could do, and he despised feeling power-less. He wanted to bring the smile back on their faces and on Marcel's, dammit.

"And you can see him?" Corinne asked Lindsey.

"I can. It doesn't mean he's dead, but it *is* linked to my abil-ity as a psychic. Will can see him, too."

Brent and Corinne turned to Will as one. "You're a psy-chic?" Brent asked.

"I didn't know until Marcel barged into our office and I could see him while Jerome couldn't. Since then, Lindsey and I have both been working with a psychic who's teaching us how to deal with this gift. But right now, our focus is on Mar-cel."

Brent rubbed his face. "This is so much." He peered at Mar-cel, even though he couldn't see him. "He's really here?"

"He is, and he's listening."

Brent took a step forward, stopping just before he passed through Marcel. "We'll find you," he promised.

The heartbreak on Marcel's face made Will want to cry.

"The psychic who's helping Lindsey and Will is also

helping us find him," Jerome intervened. "He and Marcel worked together today, and while so far, they haven't found anything, we're not losing hope. Eventually, Marcel will be able to tell us where his body is, and once he does, we'll find it and get his spirit back into it."

"So the main problem is that you don't know where Marcel's body is," Corinne said.

"From what Victor said, yes. It would also be good to know what whoever took Marcel is doing with his life energy. It can't be good, and I'm worried about that."

Will was, too. A dragon shifter had a lot more energy than a human, but it wasn't infinite. What would happen if they couldn't find Marcel in time and the person who had him took all of it?

Will didn't want to think about that possibility.

Corinne's expression shifted to stubbornness. "We'll find him," she promised. "I appreciate what this Victor person is doing, but it's not enough."

Will agreed, although without Victor, they'd have even less. It wasn't Victor's fault. He was doing everything he could, but there were other ways to find Marcel's body. Maybe they should work on both those aspects instead of focusing on Marcel finding it.

"We could bring in Timothy," Brent said.

Jerome growled. "I can't work with him," he said.

"Why not?" Lindsey asked.

"Because he's a criminal."

Will sighed. He understood where Jerome was coming from, and it was true Timothy wasn't always on the right side of the law, but he might be able to help in this situation, and Will felt that was the important part. "He's a hacker," he told Lindsey.

"He's a criminal," Jerome insisted.

Will ignored him. "When we were younger, he had a habit

of hacking into rich people's accounts and stealing their money. He redistributed it to nonprofits and people who needed help. He called himself Robin Hood, which, if you ask me, wasn't very original."

"He's a thief," Jerome insisted.

"But he's also a hacker," Will reminded him. "Besides, he doesn't do those things anymore, does he?" Will didn't have any recent contact with Timothy, but the last time they'd seen each other, Timothy's alpha found out what he was doing and had torn him a new asshole. Timothy had promised he wouldn't steal anymore, and unless he wanted to die, he'd have done just that.

"He doesn't," Corinne said. "He hasn't done anything like that for years. You can't hold what he did as a teenager against him, Jerome, especially not in a situation in which we could use him."

"How could we use him?"

"He works with computers, but I don't know what he does exactly. Still, it wouldn't hurt to ask, would it? He'll want to help Marcel get his body back."

Jerome raked a hand through his hair. "I don't think we should bring in any more people."

"Timothy's family. I also want to tell our alpha. I don't know if he'll be able to do anything, but we need to try whatever we can. I don't care what you think of Timothy. I want my son back, whatever it takes."

Jerome's shoulders slumped, and Will knew Corinne had won. He was relieved. He agreed with her that whatever they needed to do, they should do it. He didn't even care if it was illegal.

"Fine. Call Timothy," Jerome said. "But I'm not holding my breath."

"You were always unforgiving, but you should give him a chance," Corinne said softly. "He's changed, just like you have."

Jerome crossed his arms over his chest. "I haven't changed."

"Everyone changes, Jerome. That includes you, and I suspect your boyfriend has a lot to do with it."

Jerome's cheeks flushed, and he looked away. Will quite enjoyed watching his best friend with his mother, and while he felt the need to focus on Marcel, there wasn't anything they could do tonight.

"I also want to bring in Leo," Marcel said.

Lindsey related the message. Jerome's frown deepened. "You want me to tell your best friend what happened to you?"

"Someone needs to. You already told our parents, so what's one more person? We should probably set up a meeting with everyone, including Timothy and Leo, and of course, Victor. That way, we can put our heads together and think this through."

Will thought it was probably a good idea. On their own, they might not be able to find a solution, but together, things could be different.

Things *needed* to be different. They had to get Marcel out of this before it was too late.

CHAPTER FIVE

"What is he doing here?" Leo asked, glaring at Timothy. Timothy glared right back. "Marcel's my cousin. What are *you* doing here?"

"He's my best friend. Have you even talked to him recently?"

Marcel pinched the bridge of his nose. The two might not be able to see him, but they *could* give him a headache. Hopefully, Jerome would behave better, because if he started snarking at Leo and Timothy, Marcel was going to scream.

Of course, Jerome wouldn't be able to hear him, so it wouldn't change anything.

"Can we get past the moment in which you take out your dicks to find out who has the biggest one and go to work?" Lindsey asked.

Victor chuckled, and Timothy and Leo turned to glare at both of them. "Who are you?" Leo asked Lindsey.

Jerome growled. "He's my boyfriend, so you better treat him right."

Marcel and Will looked at each other. This was going to be a disaster, wasn't it? "What were we thinking?" Marcel asked.

"That we need as many people as possible to get through this," Will answered.

When Marcel looked back at his cousin and his best friend, both of them were staring at Will.

Will sighed. "Turns out I'm a psychic," he explained.

Timothy's eyes widened. "So you're talking to a ghost?" he stared at the chair in which Marcel was sitting, squinting as if trying to see him. "Who is it?"

"In this case, it's not a ghost. It's a spirit."

"I thought we were here to talk about Marcel," Leo intervened.

This was the part Marcel wasn't looking forward to. He looked at Will, who sighed and answered. "We are. Marcel is the spirit in question."

"That's not possible. He's not dead."

"He's not," Will confirmed. "But at the moment, he's not in his body, either. That's why we called both of you. We need your help."

Timothy took a seat on the other side of the table. He'd paled, but his chin had a stubborn tilt Marcel knew well. When his cousin got like this, nothing stopped him, not even the law.

"Tell us everything," Timothy ordered.

For once, Leo didn't have anything to say. He looked like he didn't believe Will, but his expression changed once Will explained what had happened to Marcel. He looked scared now, and Marcel wished he could change that. But he was scared, too, and he needed his best friend and his family.

"And you're sure he's not dead?" Leo asked once Will was done.

Victor shook his head. "I promise he's not. That might change if we don't find him soon, though."

"Because whoever is doing this to him is sucking out his life energy."

"Exactly. As a dragon shifter, Marcel has a lot of it, so hopefully, we still have a few weeks. Still, the sooner we find him, the better it'll be for him. I don't want to leave him in the hands of whoever took him one second longer than we absolutely have to."

Leo nodded. "What do you need me to do?"

Victor moved his hands as he spoke. "We have to find

Marcel's body. He's doing his best trying to locate it by himself, but his spirit isn't strong enough yet to move his body without being inside of it. He can get back to it because they're linked, but as his life energy fades, he might not be able to continue doing so."

Marcel hadn't known about that little detail, and he really wished he still didn't. It tightened the timeline even more, and it wasn't something he could afford.

"What do you need me to hack into?" Timothy asked. There was no question that this was what they needed from him and no hesitation.

Once Marcel was back in his body, he was going to hug the hell out of his little cousin.

"Marcel was able to tell us he was on a date the evening he disappeared," Lindsey said. "He remembers the guy, York, but not much else. It would be great if you could find out if the coffee shop they met at had cameras. They went on a date at a restaurant, so you could do the same there, and maybe follow Marcel's trail until he was taken."

"You're sure he's not in a hospital?" Leo asked.

"As sure as we can be. We called all the hospitals in town, and none had anyone who looks like Marcel. Besides, from what Victor told us, I doubt the kidnappers would take Marcel to a hospital. They need his life energy, and they can't steal it in a public place. No, he's somewhere else, and we need to find out where."

Leo nodded. "What can I do?"

Timothy had already taken out his computer. Marcel got to his feet to peek, but he didn't understand anything he saw on the screen. It was good to see that Timothy was already at work, though. He wanted to find Marcel as much as everyone else.

Since everyone was working, Marcel decided to try Victor's trick again. Victor and Leo were talking, their heads close together, while Lindsey was talking to Jerome. Will was still focused on Marcel, and knowing that made Marcel feel less alone. He couldn't imagine how much worse things would have been if Lindsey and Will hadn't been in Jerome's life.

The thought was terrifying.

Marcel closed his eyes and tried to breathe. Just like Victor had taught him yesterday, he focused on his body and what it felt like when he was in it. He was already getting better at centering himself and slowing down his heartbeat until the only thing he could hear was whatever happened in the room his body was in.

Then he was inside once again. It was odd, being there but not being able to do anything, not even open his eyes. He synchronized his spirit's breathing with his body's, and while it took a bit of work, it was a good thing he'd tried, because this time, he could smell things.

Marcel had never spent much time in hospitals. He was a dragon shifter, and as such, he was sturdy and didn't usually get sick. When he did, his parents contacted a healer so they wouldn't have to explain why his body was weird.

But he'd visited friends a few times, so he knew what hospitals smelled like. This was nothing like what he expected from one.

It didn't smell like disinfectant. If anything, it smelled like it hadn't been cleaned in a while. Marcel could identify mold, dust, and something that made his nose prickle. Under all of that, there was also the stench of unwashed bodies, including his own.

He continued pushing. He might not be able to open his eyes, but another sense could help identify the place.

Under all the smells, something caught his nose. It was sweet and smelled like cherry, something he was surprised to find. Since it was unexpected, he decided to focus on that. His body was unconscious, which meant someone had to be taking care of him. Maybe the cherry belonged to that person. It wouldn't help identify who it was, but it was a start, something Marcel and the others sorely needed.

It might not lead to anything, but Marcel wouldn't leave any stone unturned trying to get his body back.

Marcel had caught Will's attention. Will could tell he was trying to locate his body again, and he couldn't help but stare, hoping that this time, Marcel would have more success. But it was only the second day, so Will wasn't holding his breath. From Marcel's expression, though, something was happening, and Will was curious.

"Why are the two of you staring at the couch?" Jerome asked.

That got *everyone's* attention, even Timothy's. He looked up from his computer screen, confused, which Will understood. When he thought that he and Lindsey could see people the others couldn't, it made his head hurt.

"Marcel is trying again," Lindsey said.

Timothy swallowed. "It's still weird to think he's there."

"You get used to it after a while," Jerome grumbled.

His expression told Will he wasn't used to his brother being a spirit, though. He wanted Marcel back, as they all did.

He looked at Lindsey. He wasn't quite sure what to do. They'd talked to Victor about this yesterday, but he was just told to give Marcel time and space to do his thing. Should they ask questions? Or should they leave him to himself and hope he'd finally see something useful?

Thankfully, Victor stepped in, and Lindsey and Will didn't have to.

"Marcel?" he asked softly.

Will would have been afraid to break the moment, but it didn't seem to be a problem for Marcel. "Yeah?" he asked without opening his eyes.

"Are you in your body right now?"

"Yeah."

"Good. Can you tell us what you're seeing?"

Marcel sucked in a breath. "Nothing. I still can't open my eyes."

"That's okay. We knew it would take you a while."

"But I can smell something."

Will sat up straighter. Marcel was a shifter, and they used their other senses more than humans. Lindsey sounded hopeful, too, as he softly referred what Marcel was saying to the people in the room who couldn't hear him.

"What can you smell?" Victor asked.

He sounded excited, and when Will looked around the room, everyone seemed to share that excitement, even Jerome. Hopefully, it would lead to something instead of disappointing everyone.

"I don't think this is a hospital. It smells awful, as if there are a lot of people staying here without access to a shower."

Will wrinkled his nose. That didn't sound great. It was good to know it wasn't a hospital, though. It would also make things harder for them, because there would have been records if it had been. They'd have been able to find Marcel eventually, but in this case, they wouldn't.

"There's something else," Marcel continued. "Something smells like cherry."

That wasn't what Will expected, and, looking around, he knew he wasn't the only one.

"What kind of cherry?" Victor asked. "Is it like the fruit or something else?"

"Maybe candy?"

"That's good. Who's eating this candy?"

"Probably the guy holding my hand."

"He's still there?"

70

"Unless there's someone else holding my hand, yes. I can also hear the beeping of a heart monitor, or at least, I think that's what it is."

"It makes sense," Victor murmured. "They want to be sure you're physically okay so they can continue taking your life energy."

"Isn't there anything we can do?" Leo intervened. Lindsey was keeping up a running commentary of what Marcel was saying so everyone in the room would know.

Victor shook his head. "Unfortunately, no. Unless we find Marcel's body through Timothy, we're stuck doing it this way. Right now, Marcel is the one with the best chance at finding him."

Leo raked a hand through his hair. "I hate this."

Victor's expression had been gentle before, but it softened even more. "We all do. I promise we're doing everything we can to find Marcel."

"I'm going to try opening my eyes again," Marcel said.

Will held his breath. He wished there was more he could do for Marcel, but unfortunately, this was something Marcel had to do on his own. The only thing Will *could* do was be there for him when he came back, but even that was limited. With Marcel being a spirit, Will couldn't do anything to comfort him except talk to him.

"It's almost like my entire head is in a vat of syrup," Marcel said. "I'm struggling to do something I wouldn't even think about normally."

"Remember that it's hard for your spirit to control your body when they'd been forcefully separated," Victor said. "Just focus on what you can do, not on what's hard or impossible."

It was as if everyone in the room held their breath the way Will had been. They all stared at Marcel, or, for most of them, at where Marcel was. Jerome, Leo, and Timothy couldn't see him, but they were still there for him. They wanted him to succeed.

Marcel jerked. "It's York."

Jerome was on his feet as soon as Lindsey told him. He looked like he wanted to grab York and shake him until he told them where Marcel was.

"That's the guy you went on a date with, right?" Victor asked.

"It is. I don't understand what he's doing, though. His eyes are closed, and he's clutching my hand. It's almost as if he's doing something hard and tiring, but he's just sitting there."

Victor didn't answer. Will turned to look at him, and he wasn't the only one. Lindsey did, too, as did Timothy. Leo and Jerome kept staring at the couch where Marcel was, more interested in him. Will was interested in Marcel, too, but there was something wrong with what Marcel's date was doing to him.

"He's taking Marcel's life energy," Victor whispered.

"You can't be sure of that," Lindsey protested.

"Not a hundred percent, but I suspect that's what's going on. It would make sense that the last person Marcel remembers being with is the one hurting him."

Will's heart broke for Marcel. Marcel had told him that while he'd been interested in York, it hadn't been love at first sight, but it would still hurt him. He'd trusted York enough to be able to imagine a future with him, albeit a distant one.

"I can't do this anymore," Marcel said.

Will moved toward him, and by the time he reached the couch, Marcel's eyes were open. He looked drained, and Will desperately wanted to help him. Instead, he stood in front of him, not even sure what to say.

"You did good," Victor said.

"It doesn't feel like it. I still have no idea where my body is." Marcel rubbed his face. "And I feel like I spent the entire day in the gym."

"That's your spirit getting used to you using it this way. Get some rest."

"Is that even possible? I mean, I don't think I can sleep, can I?"

"Not in the way you think of it as a human, but you *can* rest. Try not to think about anything. Just stay on the couch, close your eyes, and rest."

Will stared at Marcel for a moment longer. He saw the moment Marcel's body relaxed, and he stepped away, not wanting to bother him. He sat back at the table, taking in Leo's frustrated expression. Jerome wasn't much different, althhough since he'd already been through this, he didn't look as shocked.

"What does all of this mean?" Timothy asked eventually.

"We don't know," Victor answered. "Marcel could be anywhere, since he's not in a hospital. It's obvious York, his date, is part of this, but we don't know how."

"I'll find him," Timothy promised.

"I have no doubt you will. Thank you."

Timothy blinked. "What for?"

"Being here. You didn't hesitate to come when your cousin needed you."

Timothy's cheeks flushed, and he looked away. "Marcel's family."

Victor nodded and tapped his fingertips onto the table. "Since there's nothing we can do now but wait, I wanted to talk to you about something," he said, turning his attention to Jerome.

Jerome frowned. "Does it have to do with Marcel?"

"It doesn't. I just noticed there's been an increase of problems with ghosts in town. Maybe it's just because I don't live here, and there have always been so many, but I was wondering."

"I haven't heard anything."

But then, they probably wouldn't have. Lindsey hadn't started working with them until recently, so most of the supernatural creatures who'd worked with them in the past knew not to come to them if they had ghost problems. Besides, Will only cared about Marcel. They could deal with whatever those ghosts were up to later once Marcel was fully back with them.

The problem was that Victor was right. None of them could do anything unless Marcel found out where his body was or Timothy found York. They couldn't just sit around and wait, and they needed to earn money. Maybe dealing with ghosts would help Will and Lindsey hone their gift. Even if it didn't, it was still something for them to do other than sitting in a chair and staring at Marcel.

CHAPTER SIX

Marcel felt like crap. He'd thought he was finally breaking through when he smelled the cherry, then managed to open his eyes and saw York, but that was all he'd been able to do, and it had been almost a week. He was terrified that his body was being drained of life energy and that by the time he got back into it, it would be only to die a second time. He didn't know how to deal with that possibility, but no matter how hard and how many times he tried to get his spirit back into it, nothing changed.

"You're frowning," Will said.

Marcel blinked and turned his attention to him. They were in Will's apartment, watching TV, or at least, they were supposed to be. Instead, Marcel was obsessing over not being good enough at this, and Will had noticed.

"Sorry. I was just thinking," he said, hoping Will wouldn't call him on it.

Together, they'd decided that Marcel would try to relax when they were home after work. He had the entire day to try to go back to his body and find out where he was, and it wouldn't help to exhaust himself. Marcel would need plenty of energy once he was able to get back to his body, which was why he'd agreed, but now, he regretted it a bit. With nothing changing, he wanted to try again and again until something finally did.

Will arched a brow. "And what were you thinking about?"

"Nothing important." Marcel stared at the TV, trying to act as if he knew what was going on in the movie they'd been watching.

"Were you thinking about how handsome I am?" Will teased.

Marcel burst out laughing. "Well, you are."

Will fluttered his lashes and pressed a hand to his heart. "Why, thank you. I can't remember the last time someone called me handsome."

"Technically, *you* called yourself handsome. I just agreed with it."

"I suppose that's right." Will's expression shifted. "Are you okay?"

Marcel sighed. Will might have been Jerome's best friend rather than Marcel's, but that didn't mean he couldn't read him. They'd known each other most of their lives, after all.

"I don't know. I hate having to wait. It's already been a week, and we still have no idea what's going on. I know Victor said that as a dragon shifter, I have a lot of life energy, but it's going to vanish eventually, and what will happen when it does?"

He knew the answer to that. He'd die, for real this time.

"You can't think that way. You can't give up."

"I don't want to, but it's hard."

It was hard for the others, too, including Will. They were as frustrated as Marcel, but they had other things to focus on. They'd gone back to work, while Marcel couldn't do anything but stare at the TV or at the wall.

"You want to try again?" Will asked, surprising Marcel.

"I thought we'd decided evenings were to relax?"

Will shrugged. "It's not like someone will arrest us if we don't relax tonight. Besides, I don't think you're relaxing. You're way too anxious about this, and maybe trying again will help."

Marcel doubted it, but he'd been thinking about doing it anyway, so he might as well. It made him feel better to know that Will would be there, watching over him, ready to intervene if something happened. Victor had shown Lindsey and Will what to do if Marcel lost himself in what he was seeing, which was terrifying when Marcel thought about it, so he tried not to.

He didn't want to lose himself in his body, not unless his spirit was attached to it again.

He nodded and closed his eyes. He could feel Will's presence next to him, and he leaned that way a bit, wanting to be closer to him.

He made the trek back to his body, something that felt almost normal by now. This, he could easily do. The problems started once he was in his body and tried to gather more information.

Sometimes, he knew he was alone in the room. He couldn't open his eyes every time, but when York was with him, he always held his hand. In the beginning, Marcel had thought it was because he cared and was worried about him, but he'd started to wonder. Victor had said that whoever had him was taking his life energy, and Marcel wondered if that was what York was doing through his hand. He didn't want to think that about York, who'd been nice and sweet when they went on that date, but he didn't truly know him.

York was holding Marcel's hand again. Marcel could feel his skin, warm and soft, but that was it. There was the smell of cherry again, too, something he'd started associating with York. York would be next to him if he opened his eyes, but he was still scared to try.

What if he failed again? He had the past few times he'd tried this, and he'd gotten back to the office with no news. Maybe the same would happen once more.

And maybe it wouldn't, and this time, Marcel would find out something more, something that could help. Even one detail could.

Marcel focused on his eyes, grinning when they opened. He blinked a few times, thinking about how strange it was to both be in his body and not. He was seeing the world through his body's eyes, but he knew he wasn't actually in the room. He was in Will's living room, with Will hovering close by.

Marcel looked down where he knew he'd find York. Sure enough, the man was there, his eyes closed, one of his hands in Marcel's. He was muttering something under his breath, and he didn't seem to notice Marcel was awake, or at least, as awake as he could be in this situation.

Marcel took the opportunity to look around. The room looked like a hospital room, but there were details that told him it wasn't. The walls were dirty, there was a giant mold patch in one corner, and there were no windows. The room was also much bigger than Marcel would have expected from a hospital, and when he looked to the side, he noticed it was divided using partitions that could have been found at a hospital but had clearly seen better days.

He turned his attention back to York. Whatever was happening, Marcel suspected his best chance to find out where he was would be to convince York to tell him. He'd have to get York's attention to make that happen, so he focused on his hand. He just needed to be able to move his fingers a tiny bit.

He grinned when he managed to squeeze York's fingers. York's eyes flew open, and he stared at Marcel in shock, his mouth gaping. "What's going on?" he asked in a whisper.

Marcel wasn't sure he could speak, but he had to try. He squeezed York's hand again, but before he could say anything, York snatched his hand away and scrambled to his feet. "This is impossible," he said. He looked around frantically as if he expected someone to walk in. "Stop that," he said with a hiss.

Marcel was about to tell him he'd stop once he found out what the fuck was going on when Will cried out. Marcel was torn, wanting to stay, and at the same time, wanting to make sure Will was okay. He stared at York for a moment longer but knew that York wouldn't talk to him even if he stayed. He was too scared, at least right now.

Marcel forced himself to leave his body. He'd be back, and next time, he'd convince York to tell him what was happening.

He blinked his eyes open and found himself in Will's living room. This time, Will wasn't sitting next to him. Instead, he was on his feet next to the couch, staring at the window. When Marcel glanced there, he realized what Will was looking at.

Two ghosts stood by the window, staring back. They were wearing modern clothes, which told Marcel they'd probably died recently, or in the past ten years anyway. He'd never seen them before, and from Will's expression, neither had he.

"I don't know who you are or what you want, but you can't be here," Will said. "You need to leave."

One of the ghosts shook his head and stepped forward, but Will thrust a hand toward him. The ghost's eyes widened, and he vanished.

The second one left, too, but Marcel couldn't tell if it was because of something Will had done or because he'd decided it was better to follow his friend. When Marcel looked at Will to check in on him, Will's eyes were wide. "I didn't know if it would work," he whispered.

"Well, it did, and you got those ghosts to leave. Well done."

Will grinned. "Thanks. What did you find out, though?"

"Nothing important." But it was still a step forward.

Even though Marcel insisted that what he'd seen didn't mean anything, Will called everyone. They hadn't seen Timothy and Leo since that first meeting, and it was time to meet up with them and find out if they'd made any progress, especially Timothy. Leo wanted to help, too, but there wasn't much he could do.

"I really don't think this was necessary," Marcel grumbled when the first person knocked on Will's door.

Will grinned at him. "Don't you want to spend time with your friends and family?"

"I do, but I can't talk to half of them."

"Just tell me if you want to say anything to anyone, and I'll help."

Will hadn't thought about how complicated Marcel's situation with his friends was. He was so used to seeing and talking to Marcel that he'd forgotten Jerome, Timothy, and Leo couldn't.

Timothy was the one who'd knocked on the door and the first one to arrive. He raised the pizza boxes he was holding and grinned. "I hope you haven't eaten yet."

Will had, but he'd never say no to pizza. "I'm sure that between all of us, there won't be one slice left by the end of the night," he said as he let Timothy in.

The others arrived soon after Timothy, and they gathered in Will's living room. Will looked around, his heart full. All of his life, he'd had Jerome and Marcel, then only Jerome. It wasn't easy for Will to make friends, and it had become harder as he aged. Now, though, he was surrounded by people, some new, some old friends, but all of them with the same goal—helping Marcel. Hopefully, they'd stay in Will's life once this was over, but even if they didn't, he was glad he'd gotten to know them.

"So, why did you call us here tonight?" Jerome asked.

"Marcel connected with his body again."

Will had pointed out the spot on the couch where Marcel was sitting, so everyone had known to leave it empty. Now, they all turned to look at it, even those who couldn't see Marcel.

"Why don't you tell them?" Marcel said. "That way, everyone will hear you."

"As long as you let me know if I make a mistake or if you have anything to add."

"I promise I will."

Will quickly went through what Marcel had told him, including the fact that Marcel had left his body when he'd heard him cry out.

"Wait, those ghosts just appeared in the middle of your living room?" Lindsey asked.

"I've never seen anything like that, but then, I've never really been in contact with ghosts." Will was curious about how those ghosts had appeared, though. From what Lindsey had told him, most of them tended to stick to places where they'd spent most of their time when they were alive. They didn't just randomly appear in strangers' living rooms.

"Can we go back to the place where Marcel's body is?" Jerome asked. He didn't sound unkind, just like he'd rather focus on his brother than on two unknown ghosts.

"I've already told you everything he told me," Will said.

"I want to go over what he saw in the room he was in again."

Will turned to look at Marcel, who shrugged.

"I already said everything I saw. It was set up like a hospital room. There was a bed with me in it and a heart monitor, as well as a chair for York. I'm pretty sure I was hooked up to some IV or something like that, but that's it. The rest of the room was nothing like a hospital. It was dark, with no windows, and smelled of dust and mold. It was also cold and damp, nothing like a hospital."

Will repeated Marcel's words, trying to think of a place that would fit. "You said the room felt big but was separated with partitions?" he asked.

"It was. I have no idea what was behind those, but I can

take a guess."

Will was horrified. So far, they'd worked on this thinking that Marcel had been the only one kidnapped, but what if he wasn't? What if someone, York or someone else, was taking life energy from more than one shifter?

"What about York?" Will asked. Jerome believed York was the one behind this, but from what Marcel had told Will about the guy, it didn't feel like it. He was involved, but that didn't mean he was the mastermind or that he didn't care about Marcel.

Marcel frowned. "He wasn't like I remembered him. I mean, even when we met, he was really thin, like maybe he didn't eat enough. We went on that date just a little under a week after that, and in that week, he changed. He freaked out when I opened my eyes. He looked terrified, and that's not all. I don't think he'd had a shower recently, not from the state his hair was in, and he looked even worse. I'm pretty sure he's not eating at all now."

This time, Lindsey repeated Marcel's words so the others could know what he'd said. Will was focused on York, wondering what was up with the guy.

If he was scared and hadn't been eating, maybe he'd been kidnapped, too. Maybe whoever had taken Marcel hadn't intended to take York, but since they'd been together, they had. Or perhaps York was involved, but not willingly.

There were a lot of possibilities, but he couldn't explore any of them without knowing who York was.

Will looked at Timothy. "Do you have any news about York?"

Timothy's mouth was full, but he quickly swallowed, cleaned his mouth, and nodded. "Something, although not much. The restaurant didn't have cameras, so I wasn't able to find anything, but the coffee shop did. I found footage of their meeting, and I managed to grab a picture of York. It's not great, though."

"Can you send them to our phones?" Jerome asked.

Timothy's phone was in his hand before Jerome was done speaking. His fingers flew on the screen, and a few seconds later, Will's phone vibrated on the coffee table. He snatched it up and unlocked it to look at the picture Timothy had sent to everyone in the room.

He hadn't been wrong when he'd said it wasn't great. All Will could see of York was that he was short, very thin, and blond.

"This isn't helpful," Jerome said with a growl.

"Maybe I could help?" Leo intervened. "I could draw York if Marcel and one of the psychics help me."

Will's eyes widened. "You draw?"

"And he's pretty good at it," Marcel said. "I think it's a good idea. It's obvious we won't get anything from the cameras, so this might be the best way for us to find him."

"I'll help," Lindsey volunteered.

The three of them gathered in the kitchen. Will dug out some paper and a pencil from his desk in the guest room and left them to it after giving them to Leo. When he went back to the living room, he found that Victor and Timothy were talking. Timothy was on his phone while Victor looked over his shoulder. That left Jerome, who was sitting on the couch, still staring at the spot where his brother had been sitting until now.

Will joined him. "He's not there anymore," he said, teasing.

"I know. It's still odd to think that he's here and I can't see him." Jerome looked at Will. "And what if one day, he's not there anymore?"

"We'll do everything we can to help him." Will wanted to promise everything would be all right, but he couldn't. He wouldn't lie to his best friend.

"I know." Jerome rubbed his face. "How about you? How

are you dealing with this psychic thing?"

"I'm fine. I'm just worried about Marcel."

For some reason, Jerome looked surprised. "I know the two of you were friends when we were kids, but it's been a while since you saw each other, isn't it?"

"Maybe, but it doesn't mean we're not close. He's been living with me, after all."

"I suppose." Jerome still didn't look convinced, but Will did care about Marcel, and he hadn't been lying when he said he'd do everything he could. He couldn't imagine a life without Marcel in it, even if they never saw each other again after this was over.

Marcel had never done anything like this, but he'd watched Leo draw thousands of times. He knew how good his best friend was, and he hoped it meant they'd be able to find York. He felt like it might be the only way for Marcel to get out of this, and time was running out.

He peered at the drawing Leo was making. "His jaw is a bit softer," he said.

It was awkward to have Lindsey repeat everything Marcel was saying, but at least they'd found a way to make this work. Marcel wished he could speak to his best friend without someone in the middle of the conversation, but he supposed he could keep in the emotional stuff until he was back in his body.

What if he never was, though? How would he tell Leo he loved him?

Jerome had Will, and while Will and Marcel had been friends, Marcel had never been as close to him as he was to Leo. It had always been that way. Leo was a few years older than Marcel, and when they were teenagers, it felt like a lot. They'd gone to the same high school, but Leo and his parents had belonged to the dragon clan, which put more space between them. They were still clan members, while Marcel had never been a clan member. That hadn't stopped them from being friends when they'd met again in college, and now, Leo was the best friend Marcel ever had.

As Leo continued drawing, Lindsey leaned closer to Marcel. "Can I ask you something?"

"You already did," Marcel pointed out. "But sure. Let's hear it."

"Is there something between you and Will?"

That got Leo's attention. "I've been wondering that, too, but it's harder for me to understand because I can't see or talk to Marcel."

"We're friends," Marcel told them. "That's all there is to it."

"Are you sure? Because I know you've been friends for a long time, but what I see between the two of you feels different," Lindsey said. "Not that it's a problem if the two of you are only friends, of course. I'm just curious, because it's obvious Will cares about you a lot, and you care about him."

"It would be great if the two of you could find each other through this situation," Leo added.

Marcel had both of them focused on him now, but he still wasn't sure how to answer Lindsey's question.

Yes, he and Will had been friends almost their entire life. Yes, he cared about Will more than he cared about a lot of people. Did that mean he had a crush on Will? He didn't know. They'd been spending time together because of the situation, and it had helped Marcel discover Will again. He was glad he had, but he couldn't help but wonder what Will would do if Marcel ended up dying. Could they really start a relationship when Marcel was still a spirit and had no guarantee he'd ever get back to his body?

Marcel was thinking about protecting Will. He didn't want Will to get hurt, not if he could help it. He supposed that answered Lindsey's question, at least in part.

Marcel could easily fall in love with Will. With everything else, he hadn't realized it was already happening, but now, Lindsey had forced him to think about it, and he knew.

He *was* falling in love with Will.

Will had always been a friend, but Marcel was seeing him in a different light. Will was a caring man who didn't have to be involved in this situation but had decided to be because he cared about an old friend. He'd opened his home to Marcel when he hadn't had to, and they'd been spending every evening together, watching TV and talking. He'd supported Marcel through all of this — even when Marcel didn't have faith in himself. Will's faith in him had never wavered.

Marcel sighed. "Maybe I do have a crush on him." It was an understatement. He'd always loved Will. That love was changing, but it was still there.

Lindsey grinned. "I knew it."

"What?" Leo asked, eager to be part of the conversation.

"He admitted he has a crush on Will."

Marcel raised his hands. "Don't start planning the wedding. I do like Will as more than a friend, even though I hadn't realized it, but nothing can come out of this."

Lindsey frowned. "Why not?"

"Because I don't want to hurt him. What will happen if this situation ends badly? We're trying to find a way for me to get back into my body, but we might not manage. What if I die? What if Will and I get together only for him to lose me? I don't want to do that to him."

Lindsey quietly repeated Marcel's words to Leo, who nodded. "But what if you *do* get back to your body?" Leo asked. "What if Will is what you need to be stronger and have more faith in yourself? I can't talk with you, but I know you. I know how heavily this is weighing on you. You're losing hope, and I don't want that. Maybe Will is the thing you need to continue believing you'll make it out. Besides, with every-thing going on, you need something good in your life."

Marcel swallowed and looked down at the drawing. He'd thought he'd found something good with York, but that had been a mess. He obviously shouldn't have trusted York, and he wasn't sure he could trust anyone else after this.

But Will was different. Marcel knew him almost as well as he knew his brother. Will would never hurt him or betray him. Was there anyone more perfect for Marcel than him?

Marcel sighed and tilted his chin toward the drawing. "His hair is longer," he said.

Lindsey stared for a moment before nodding and telling Leo what Marcel had said. For some reason, Leo looked amused, but he didn't push. Marcel was grateful because he needed time to think.

He wanted to be with Will but felt selfish at the thought of doing something in that direction. Of course, he didn't know if Will wanted to be with him that way, but it would be fairly easy to find out. Marcel had never had a problem asking peo-ple out, figuring that rejection was better than watching them from afar and wondering what could happen.

Will wouldn't hurt him, even if he rejected him. He'd be gentle and sweet about it, and they'd stay friends.

What would happen if Will *did* want to date Marcel? What if they got closer and Marcel eventually died? That was some-thing else Marcel had to deal with, and he wasn't sure he had the capacity to do that at the moment. He didn't know how to deal with his own death, even though it was becoming clearer every day that he might just have to.

But Leo was right. Maybe Marcel needed something good to keep hope alive, and this was perfect. *Will* was perfect, and now that he'd started thinking about it, Marcel couldn't stop. He could imagine he and Will together, and he couldn't wait to find out if it could become a reality.

If it couldn't, he'd deal with it. If it could and he realized he was going to die, he'd deal with that, too. He wouldn't be doing it alone like he'd been trying to do.

He'd have Will.

Will flopped onto the couch, relieved that everyone had left. He'd been happy to have friends over for one evening, but he was exhausted, and he was glad he and Marcel were alone now.

Once he was done, Leo had snapped a picture of the drawing he'd made of York and had sent it to everyone. Will had been impressed, especially when Marcel had said it was a pretty good rendition of the guy. York had looked tired in the drawing, which was how Marcel had described him, especially when he'd seen him in the room he was being kept in. Now they knew what York looked like, but they still didn't know where to find him or if they could. It was a worry Will wasn't ready to deal with today, though. He was too tired for that.

Marcel settled on the couch next to Will.

It was going on midnight, so Will would go to bed soon, but he wanted a little time with Marcel first. Marcel looked so sad that Will wished he could hug him. He wanted to do something to comfort his friend, and okay, maybe he also wanted to know how Marcel would feel against him.

Will had never been attracted to Jerome, but Marcel was different. They hadn't been as close, and Will had always found him handsome. He still did, even more than before. Marcel had been a cute teenager, but he was a gorgeous man—one Will was starting to realize he might not know as well as he had the teenage Marcel. That wasn't surprising, but the fact that he wanted to know more was.

"Nothing has changed," Marcel murmured.

"Now we know what York looked like. You heard Timothy. He's going to try to put the drawing into a facial recognition software and see what comes out." Will had wanted to ask how he'd gotten that software, but he'd been worried about the answer, so he hadn't. If Timothy did anything illegal, Will didn't want to know about it. "Hopefully, he'll find York."

Marcel nodded. "What if he doesn't?"

"If he doesn't, well, you'll continue visiting your body until you're strong enough to find out where you are or maybe to convince York to let you go."

Marcel looked at Will. "What if we can't do this in time? What if I die?"

That wasn't something Will never wanted to think about, but Marcel did, more often every day. "Then you'll die surrounded by your friends and people who love you," he whispered. "I can't imagine being in your place, and I understand it's hard for you not to think about what will happen if we can't find you, but there's still hope. We're all working on this, and I *know* we'll find you."

Marcel was still staring, but Will couldn't tell what he was thinking. That was why he was stunned when instead of continuing to talk about his possible death, Marcel said, "I wish I could kiss you."

Will licked his lips. "Is that something you want?" They were leaning closer to each other, even though they couldn't touch.

"I do. I don't know when it happened, but I'd *really* like to kiss you."

Their lips were close now, so close that if Marcel had been in his body, they would have brushed against each other. Will would have been able to feel Marcel's breath on his lips, and they would have kissed.

But they couldn't. No matter how much Will wanted to try,

he already knew what would happen if he did.

He chuckled. "Raincheck?"

Marcel stared for a moment longer before leaning back and nodding. "I'll hold you to that."

"I want you to. I plan to kiss you until you can't breathe once you're in your body again." Will hesitated. "What about York?"

"Well, even if he has nothing to do with what's happening to me, I don't think I could date him again. I'll always associate him with this, and it would be hard to get over. Besides, it was only a first date. I wanted to see where things could go, but I'm fine never finding out."

"But you want to see where things go between the two of us?"

"I do. I've always had feelings for you, but I didn't realize they'd started to change recently. It's only been a week, but it's like you've been in my life all this time, and I have *strong* feelings for you. I know this is far from the ideal moment to say this, and I'm probably freaking you out, but if I die, I want you to know I was serious about us."

Will wanted to scream that Marcel wouldn't die, but he didn't. If Marcel needed this, Will would let him have it.

"You're not freaking me out," he said instead. "I've always felt strongly about you, too. I'm glad we found each other again and that we'll try dating once this is over. There's no one I trust more with my heart than you."

"Even though I could break it soon?"

"Even if you do break it, it won't be your fault. So yes, I trust you with my heart." But unfortunately, Marcel was right when he said this wasn't the right moment to do this. They couldn't touch, and they couldn't kiss. Even worse, there was always the fear that Marcel wouldn't survive. It probably wasn't smart for Will to get close to Marcel, but he didn't care about smart. He cared about Marcel and making him happy, especially if these were their last days together.

But Will didn't want to think about that. He forced himself to smile and leaned closer to Marcel, even though they couldn't touch. He turned the TV back on and snuggled one of the pillows on the couch to his chest, trying to convince himself it was Marcel.

They stayed silent for a while, but it didn't last. It never did between them, although Will was relieved when they didn't start talking about York and what was happening to Marcel again. Instead, they chatted about their favorite TV shows and movies, and it was a hint of the normalcy they could have together once this was over.

Will wanted it. He wanted all of it with Marcel, and he prayed he'd get it even as his eyelids grew heavy and he started falling asleep. He should go to bed, but he felt so good here with Marcel that instead, he allowed sleep to claim him.

CHAPTER SEVEN

Everyone was busy. Marcel didn't know what happened, but suddenly, his brother's PI agency had been taken over by clients. They kept coming over and calling, looking bewildered and, in some cases, scared. It was so bad that Victor, Leo, and even Timothy, were helping, although in Leo and Timothy's case, there wasn't much they could do except talk to the clients and write down their story for the others to go over later.

All the clients were here because of ghosts.

Victor had been right when he'd said something was happening in town with the ghosts, but they'd been able to ignore it until now. Jerome had believed the people affected wouldn't come to them because they didn't usually deal with ghosts, but he'd been wrong. They were lucky that Victor was with them and that Will had found out he was a psychic, but even with three of them, they were having trouble keeping up.

Marcel stared at the ceiling and listened to the voices ringing in the office. He was in the break room, but it had become Victor's office, which meant Marcel couldn't find peace even here. At the moment, Victor was talking to a woman in tears about something a ghost did in her house. Marcel was sorry for her, but with everyone busy, it meant his problem had slid to the back burner, and he didn't feel he had that kind of time.

Everyone wanted to work on finding him. They still were, in between clients, early in the morning and late at night, and during their lunch break. They were all exhausted, and

Marcel felt guilty, something he didn't like. His brother and the others needed to earn money to survive, and maybe he was being selfish by wanting them to focus on him, but he didn't feel he had much time left. What would happen when his life energy ran out? He never wanted to find out, so the fact that no one could help was a problem.

Marcel needed to do more.

At this point, he'd realized it would be on him to save his body, and that was fine with him. He shouldn't have relied on everyone else, because it wasn't right. He was the one in trouble, and he'd get himself out of it.

He got to his feet. Victor's gaze briefly flickered toward him, but his attention turned back to the woman he was talking to almost right away. That was fine with Marcel, who left the break room and went to look for a quiet place. He'd slip out the back room if he had to and sit on the ground. He wouldn't be able to focus with so many people talking and crying in the office, but no one had said he needed to stay here. He had until now because he hadn't wanted to be away from Will and Jerome and because he didn't really have another place to go, but he was ready to leave.

Thankfully, he didn't need to go. He peeked in Will's office, but the man was nowhere to be seen. He waited for a moment, wanting to see if Will came back with a client, but he didn't. He was probably in Jerome's office talking to someone, and Marcel took advantage of it and slipped in.

With some effort and focus, he closed the door behind himself, hoping it would help keep everyone away for a moment. Victor had explained that for ghosts, some things like sitting in a chair were routine, so they could do it without too much effort. But other things, like moving objects or touching someone, weren't. That meant ghosts had to focus, and the longer they'd been dead, the easier it was. Marcel's situation was different because he wasn't dead, yet at the same time, it was similar.

Once he'd managed to close the door, he sat on the couch in the corner, made himself as comfortable as possible considering the couch was shit and it felt like sitting on a rock, and closed his eyes.

He *was* going to talk to York today, dammit.

There was so much noise around him that it took him a moment to be able to focus enough to find his body. Once he did, he sucked in a breath, then waited a moment to get used to it again. The sensation of being there, yet not, never became less strange, and he couldn't wait to be permanently back in his body.

He was never leaving it again once he was.

Marcel took a deep breath and opened his eyes. He couldn't feel York holding his hand today, so he was surprised to find him sitting in the chair next to the bed. York was frowning and sucking on something, maybe one of those cherry candies Marcel now associated with him. He was staring into the distance, and Marcel waited a moment to see if he'd noticed what was happening. When he didn't, Marcel knew he had to get his attention.

He prayed York wouldn't freak out the way he had the other day.

Marcel tried to speak, but that was too much for him, and when he opened his mouth, only a croak came out. Thankfully, it was enough to make York look up. His eyes widened, and he jerked out of his chair, but this time, he didn't freak out as badly as he had a few days ago.

He stared at Marcel as if trying to understand what was going on. Marcel wanted to find out, too. He wanted answers, and he wanted them *now*, but the problem was that he wasn't in shape to ask questions. That wouldn't stop him, so he opened his mouth and tried asking what the fuck was going on again. "York," was the only thing that came out of his mouth.

York's eyes widened. "What the fuck?" he asked in a whisper.

"York," Marcel repeated. "What are you doing?"

It was getting easier to speak, but Marcel still sounded like Frankenstein's monster. His voice was slow and, honestly, scary. If someone had talked to him this way in a dark alley, he'd have run the other way. It was a small miracle York hadn't yet, although maybe it was because he was rooted in place with fear. He certainly looked like that was the case.

York shook his head. "This is impossible," he said.

"What's impossible?"

"You shouldn't be able to open your eyes, let alone talk to me."

He looked around, and Marcel remembered he'd done the same thing last time. It was as if he was afraid someone was going to walk in on them.

York looked worse every time Marcel saw him. He clearly wasn't getting enough food or sleep—maybe none at all. He certainly didn't look like it, what with his too-long hair hanging around his face greasy and dirty, his cheeks sunken in his face, and his eyes that looked wider than they should because of how thin his face had become. His jeans hung on his slim body, and his t-shirt looked like he'd borrowed it from his big brother. His nails were dirty, as if he hadn't washed his hands in a while.

York rubbed them on his thighs. "What's going on?" he asked in a whisper.

"I was going to ask you the same thing," Marcel said slowly. "What happened to me? What are you doing? Where am I?"

York shook his head. "You don't understand. He's going to kill you and me if he finds out you're awake. How is it possible? The spell he has you under is still working, so you

95

shouldn't be awake."

Marcel wasn't about to explain he wasn't. He was more interested in the *he* York had just mentioned. "Who's going to kill you?"

York shook his head and pushed strands of dirty hair away from his face. "I can't tell you. You need to act as if you're still under his spell. They're going to hurt you otherwise."

"Tell me where we are, York. I can get you out with me, but I need to know what's happening and where we are."

"You won't be able to do anything. He's too strong."

"We can at least try. I know you don't want to do whatever it is you're doing."

York looked away and took a step back. "I never wanted to hurt anyone," he whispered.

Which meant he knew he was hurting Marcel. Marcel was angry, even though he could tell it was obvious York wanted nothing to do with the situation. It wouldn't be enough for him to stop pushing. He wanted answers, and now that he had the opportunity, he was going to get them.

Or at least he hoped so.

Will was surprised to find his office door closed when we went back to it. He'd walked a new client to the front door after talking to her about her son's ghost, who'd started appearing in her house and throwing fits so bad that he'd managed to hit her in the forehead with a glass. Luckily, she hadn't been hurt badly, but she could have, and she'd been scared. Will understood, and he was happy to help her—or he would have been in any other situation.

Right now, he had too many people to help and not enough hours in the day to do it.

Even with Victor's help, they were overwhelmed. Will had no idea what was going on with the ghosts, and honestly, he didn't care. He just wanted this to be over so they'd be able to focus on Marcel.

Will smiled. That was why his office door was closed. Marcel was no doubt inside, trying to locate his body. He hadn't said anything about the fact that everyone was busy working, but they all knew time was running out. They needed to find Marcel's body, and since no one else was able to work on it, Marcel had decided to do it on his own.

Will was careful when he opened the office door. He didn't want to do something that would distract Marcel if he was in his body, but he was curious. He gently pushed open the door, his eyes widening when he heard Marcel talking to someone. He didn't have to look to know the office was empty except for Marcel. That meant he was talking to someone who wasn't here — hopefully, York.

Since Marcel was busy, Will didn't go inside. Instead, he hovered by the cracked door and listened.

"You need to calm down," Marcel told the person he was talking to. Will couldn't hear the answer, which was frustrating, to say the least. He wanted to step in and be there to support Marcel, but the best thing he could do at the moment was to stay where he was.

"I don't understand what you're saying," Marcel continued. "You're afraid of whoever this guy is, but I can't help you if you don't tell me what's going on. I'm not doing this alone. Even if I'm unable to do anything, I have other people who will help you. I promise."

Will gritted his teeth. If Marcel was talking to York, it didn't sound like it was going well. Will wanted to scream at the unfairness of everything, but instead, he turned around and went to knock on Jerome's office. He quickly explained what was going on without giving too many details, since Jerome was with a client, then left that office and went to Lindsey's. The next one was Victor, and by the time Will was done talking to all of them, they'd started ushering the clients out. They wanted to be ready in case they had to head out and get Marcel's body. Hopefully, he was talking some sense into York.

Once Will was done telling everyone what was happening, he went to stand in front of his office door. He wouldn't put it past Jerome or Leo to barge in and break Marcel's focus, which they couldn't afford, since this sounded like it was going decently well.

"Why are we here and not inside?" Timothy asked in a whisper.

"Just listen," Will said.

He pushed the door open just a bit more.

"I just want to know what's happening," Marcel was saying in a soft voice. "I thought you liked me. Why are you doing this?"

There was a pause, and Timothy looked at Will with wide eyes. "I have no idea what's going on."

Will almost laughed. For a moment, he'd forgotten that Timothy couldn't hear Marcel. "I think he's talking to York. He's telling him that he'll help York if someone is hurting him. York seems to be afraid, though, so I don't know if it'll work."

"I hate not being able to hear anything," Timothy grumbled.

Will could understand that. "I get it—I can only hear Marcel, and it's incredibly frustrating."

Timothy snorted. "At least you can hear *something*."

Will supposed he was right. He'd never regretted finding out he was a psychic, but in cases like this one, he was glad for it. If he hadn't been a psychic, he wouldn't have been able to be here for Marcel and to hear or see him.

The others started arriving, and while no one asked what was going on, Will could see Jerome wanted to go in. He shook his head. Jerome huffed but obeyed and stayed where he was, with Lindsey leaning closer to tell him what Marcel was saying.

When everything was quiet in the office for a few minutes, Will pushed the door open and peeked in. Marcel was still on the couch in the same position, but he was silent. He looked almost stuck, and for a moment, Will was afraid that was what had happened. He rushed to Marcel's side, wanting to bring him back.

He crouched in front of Marcel. "Marcel?" he asked softly.

Marcel blinked. It obviously took him a moment to see Will, even though Will was right in front of him. Then his shoulders relaxed, and he leaned forward, reaching out for Will's cheek.

"What's happening now?" Jerome asked.

"Your brother's back," Victor told him.

Will was staring at Will and Marcel with a smile. He had no doubt that Victor knew something was going on between them, but he didn't mind. He wasn't ashamed of being in love with Marcel. He just hoped they'd have the opportunity to be together as a couple instead of having to keep their hands to each other because they couldn't touch.

"Well? What happened?" Jerome asked.

Will got to his feet. Marcel still looked bewildered and like he wasn't quite sure where he was, which Will supposed made sense, since he'd just had an out-of-body experience.

Well, kind of.

"Give him a moment," he told Jerome. "I'm sure he'll answer every question you have, but this can't have been easy. I heard him talking to someone, and I think it was York."

Jerome's eyes widened, and he took a step forward only to stop and nod. "We'll wait for as long as he needs," he promised.

Will knew they would, but he hoped it wouldn't be too

long. They didn't have a lot of time left, and they needed something, *anything* that would lead them to Marcel. Hopefully, Marcel had at least a few answers now that he'd spoken to York. Will wasn't sure what they'd do if he didn't.

Marcel was bewildered. He felt he needed to go back to his body, but also like he didn't truly belong in it. It was an odd sensation, and it was even weirder to be here and see Will in front of him. Marcel had been talking to York until a few moments ago. He'd been in another room, in another building. Hopefully, he hadn't been in another town, but he couldn't swear on it.

He rubbed at his face. "I'm fine," he promised.

Will didn't look convinced. "Take all the time you need."

Marcel wanted to, but they didn't *have* time. He wasn't sure if what he'd gotten from York could help, and he wouldn't find out until he told the others and they could work on it together.

They were a team, and they were all waiting for Marcel to explain.

He sucked in a breath and turned his attention to their little group. "I talked to York," he said.

Lindsey had become Marcel's mouthpiece when they were all together, and he quickly told the others what Marcel had just said. Jerome stepped forward as if he wanted to grab Marcel and wrap him into his arms, and Marcel yearned for him to do just that. Since it wouldn't happen, he focused on what had.

"I don't know what's going on with him, but he's getting worse. I'm surprised he didn't faint when he saw me, to be honest. He looked like he might. He was so pale that I could have mixed him up with a ghost. We need to do something to help him."

"We have to focus on you first," Will said, his voice uncompromising. "I understand you want to help him, and I don't have anything against that, but you come first."

Marcel nodded. "I agree. I just want everyone to know I'm not leaving him behind. I promised we could help him, and I have every intention of doing just that if I have the opportunity."

"Tell us what he said," Victor demanded.

Marcel closed his eyes, hoping it would help him remember every single word and every detail.

"He wasn't holding my hand this time. I think that when he does, it's because he's taking my life energy. Today, he was there because I was awake the last time he saw me, and he wanted to see if it happened again. He freaked out when it did, especially when I started talking. I expected him to run out of the room, but he stayed where he was. He was frantic."

"Because it takes a strong soul and spirit to be able to do what you just did," Victor murmured.

Marcel shrugged. He didn't feel strong. He felt desperate and like his time was running out. "He's afraid of someone. He kept saying that person was going to kill both of us, and it's obvious that whoever this is, they're forcing him to do all of this. He might be taking my life energy, but he's not doing it because he wants to. Someone took him, just like they took me."

Marcel wasn't sure that was the entire truth. York had said he'd never meant to hurt anyone, and Marcel believed that. That didn't mean he wasn't doing it, although whether it was because he was afraid the guy who was somehow controlling him and Marcel would hurt him or because of something else, Marcel couldn't say.

"I think we can convince him to help me," he added.

"You still don't know where your body is?" Leo asked after Lindsey told everyone what Marcel had just said.

Marcel would be glad when he didn't need someone to talk for him anymore. "I don't. I was able to look better at the room around me, but it hadn't changed. It's obviously not a hospital, and while I don't know how big it is, I don't think it was a home, abandoned or not. The room was too big."

"Can you give us an approximation of the size of the place?" Victor asked. "It doesn't need to be precise, but it could help us understand where to focus."

Marcel shook his head. "I have no clue. I think I can convince York to tell me, though. I want to go back right now and try."

Victor opened his mouth, but whatever he was about to say never crossed his lips.

A ghost suddenly appeared in the middle of the office. She blinked and looked around, her gaze stopping on Marcel. Marcel had never seen her before, and he didn't know who she was or what she wanted. He steeled himself, wondering if she was about to attack him, but instead, she grinned wickedly and reached for Will's laptop.

Luckily, Will noticed it and grabbed it before she could. He held it close to his chest, and since the ghost couldn't take it, she had to make do with the empty coffee mug on the desk. She grabbed it and threw it at the wall, shards of ceramic going everywhere.

Leo, Jerome, and Timothy looked around with wide eyes. They couldn't see the ghost, but they could see what she was doing, at least in part.

The next thing to go was a frame on the wall. It flew through the room, breaking against the other wall. Marcel had no idea what was going on, so he turned to the experts.

"Why is she doing this?" he asked Victor.

Victor shook his head. "I don't know."

"I don't want to be rude, but I think she's just a bitch," Lindsey said.

Marcel looked at him.

Lindsey shrugged. "What? She wouldn't be the first bitchy ghost I've met. She probably wants something and is unhappy we're not giving her attention."

He might be right, but it would make more sense if the ghost had asked for something. She hadn't, so how did she expect them to help her?

"You'll pay for this," she said.

Marcel had no idea what she was talking about, and from the puzzled expressions on the others' faces, he wasn't the only one.

To his surprise, Will raised his hands and moved closer to her, ignoring Lindsey when he reached to stop him. "Hello," he said.

The woman turned toward Will. Her eyes narrowed. "Leave us alone," she snapped.

"I'm sorry, but I don't know what you're talking about."

She grinned. "Oh, but you do, and you'll regret it. Stay away from us. If you don't, you'll be the first to die."

Marcel did *not* like the way this conversation was going. "I don't know who I'm supposed to stay away from. Why don't you tell me?" he intervened.

Instead of answering, the woman grabbed the mug Will kept his pens and pencils and threw it at Will's head. Thankfully, Jerome snatched him and pulled him back, and the mug hit the wall, ceramic and pens raining down.

"What the fuck is going on?" Jerome asked with a growl.

"I don't know. She's threatening us and telling us to stay away from *them*, but I don't know who she's talking about." Marcel couldn't watch Will get hurt, but he also couldn't do anything.

The woman pointed a finger at Will's face. "You *know* what I'm talking about. We won't allow you to take him from us."

With that, she disappeared.

Everyone in the office stayed silent and still for a moment. Will relaxed. His shoulders slumped, and that seemed to be the signal the people who couldn't see ghosts needed.

"That was awesome," Timothy breathed out.

Marcel wanted to throttle him. Didn't he realize how much danger Will had been in?

Jerome scowled at him. "Awesome? She almost killed Will."

"She threw a mug at his head. It wouldn't have killed him."

"He's human, dickhead. Even if he hadn't died, he could have been hurt."

Timothy looked chastised, but Marcel didn't care. He was still thinking about the woman's last words. *We won't allow you to take him from us.*

Who had she been talking about? The only thing that made sense was that she'd been talking about him, but could it be possible? York and whoever he was working for needed shifters to take their life energy, and ghosts didn't have life energy anymore. Could they use ghosts as soldiers? Or was this woman also working with York's boss and warning them to stay away?

Marcel had hoped they'd have more answers by the time he was done talking to York, but instead, they had more questions than ever.

Will was exhausted.

Once the ghost had left, he'd put his office back together. After that, he, Victor, and Lindsey had sat down to work on their psychic gifts some more. They could have used them to push the ghost away earlier, but Will hadn't even thought about it, and that wouldn't do. He was a psychic, and he had to deal with ghosts. He needed to remember what he could do in this kind of situation instead of trying to solve it using his words like he usually did.

But everyone was fine. What the woman had said made everyone worry, mostly because it meant that whoever had taken Marcel wasn't working on their own. Marcel had mentioned it was probably a guy, from the way York talked about him, but if he wasn't alone, they could be facing anyone, and they wouldn't know until they were in front of them.

"You should call your mother," Timothy said.

Will blinked. He'd been dozing off on the couch in the break room, and he wasn't sure who Timothy was talking to. "I'm sorry?"

Timothy, who was at the table working on his computer, shrugged. "I was telling Marcel he should call his mother."

Will had to repress a smile. "He's not here at the moment."

Timothy groaned. "This is so freaking weird. I thought I was talking to him, and I didn't want to be rude by telling you to tell him he should call his mother."

"He went to talk to Victor. I can ask him to come back if you want?"

Timothy waved Will's words away. "It's fine. But she's looking for York, too, along with the entire clan. That's why I was saying that Marcel should call her. He has a bit more information about York now, and I'm sure Corinne would want to know about the ghost who attacked us earlier."

"You're still thinking about her words."

Lindsey had told everyone what the ghost had said once she'd vanished. They were understandably worried, but they hadn't talked about it yet. They would have to, but Will didn't have the energy, not today.

Timothy frowned. "Especially the last words. It was obvious she was talking about Marcel, and that doesn't bode well. What did she say again? That she and her friends won't allow us to take him from them?"

Will nodded. "Exactly that. And yes, I'm worried about it, too. We already knew that whatever they were using Marcel's life energy for, it couldn't be good, but this makes everything more ominous. They have plans, and they don't want us to intervene. I don't know what they're ready to do to make sure we don't, but I'm not looking forward to finding out."

"I agree. I've been doing everything I can to find York, but even with the drawing, it's almost impossible. I'm looking through driver's licenses at the moment, but if he doesn't have one, I might not find him."

And even if they did find York, there was nothing to say he'd agree to help them.

Marcel believed that York wasn't willingly working for the people who'd taken him, but Will still wasn't sure. He wondered if it was because York had been on a date with Marcel, and now, he and Marcel were planning to date. Maybe he was just jealous of York, but he didn't think that was the case. Still, perhaps he could ask Timothy, just to be sure.

"You know that Marcel believes York is doing this against his will," he started.

Timothy nodded. "I'm not sure if it's because he likes the guy or because he truly believes that. I mean, he's the only one of us who's seen York sucking his life energy. Maybe York is a great actor, or maybe Marcel is right. There's no way for us to know."

"So you don't trust York."

Timothy snorted. "I don't trust anyone but the people who are here today and the dragon clan. Hell, I don't even trust everyone in the clan. I do think that whether or not York is willingly doing this matters, but at the moment, I don't care. I just want Marcel back, and I don't think we have a lot of time left to make that happen. If we manage to get York out of the situation while also grabbing Marcel, that's great. If we can only take one of them, though, I know who I'm choosing, and it's not the guy who took my cousin on a date before kidnapping him."

Will relaxed. It wasn't just because he was jealous, then.

He shouldn't have doubted himself. He had feelings for Marcel, but he was also an experienced PI. The psychic thing was new, but everything else was still the same. It was hard to judge York without meeting him, but Will knew about York's actions. That was something he *could* judge him on, and he didn't like what he knew.

He could understand York being forced to do something like this, though. He'd easily agree to anything if someone took Jerome or Marcel and threatened them if he didn't do what they wanted. He hoped he'd never be in that kind of situation, but if he was, their lives came before the life of someone he didn't know. Maybe that was what York was working with. Maybe he'd had to choose between the life of a loved one, or even his own, and Marcel's. Could Will or anyone else blame him for that?

Will's answer was *no*, but he didn't know if it would stay the same once he met York. He supposed he'd see, and, like Timothy, he wouldn't think twice about saving Marcel before anyone else.

Marcel came into the room, hesitating when he saw Will and Timothy alone. "Am I interrupting something?"

"Timothy and I were talking about York," Will explained. When Timothy blinked at him, he gestured in Marcel's direction. "Marcel is here."

"Good. I also told Will you should call your mother."

Marcel groaned. "Do I really have to?"

"The clan is working on finding York, and you have new information about him. I'm sure they want to hear all of it, as well as what we suspect is happening."

Marcel scowled. "And what do we suspect is happening?"

Will straightened. "Someone is forcing psychics to take the life energy from shifters. They're apparently working with ghosts, or at the very least, one of them. I also suspect that whatever they're doing is causing unrest in the ghost population in town. It might just be a coincidence, but I doubt that's the case."

"You think that whoever took Marcel is using the ghosts?" Timothy asked.

"I don't know. I'm not even sure it's possible, although I suppose he could convince some of the ghosts to work with him, create trouble so we'll stay away from Marcel. And it's worked. We've been focusing on our job the past few days while we wait until Marcel or you find York. Maybe that's what these people wanted."

And they'd fallen right into that trap. Now that they knew about it, it was over. Will didn't care if the entire town was overrun with ghosts. Marcel came first, and Will would sacrifice his job if he had to in order to make sure Marcel was safe.

When he looked at Timothy, he knew he wasn't the only one. Timothy's expression was hard, and his fingers were flying on his keyboard. He was still looking for York, and Will had no doubt that Timothy wouldn't stop for anything or anyone.

Hopefully, no one would get hurt by one of the ghosts going nuts. Will would feel guilty if that happened, and he suspected Marcel would feel the same. But it would be even worse if they couldn't get to Marcel in time, and that wasn't an option Will was ready to contemplate, no matter how Marcel felt.

They were saving him, and that was final.

CHAPTER EIGHT

M arcel peered into Will's bedroom, feeling like a creep for watching him sleep. He wanted to reassure himself that Will was okay. Logically, he'd known Will was, but everything happening was taking a toll on him emotionally. Marcel was terrified for his life, terrified that something would happen to Will or one of their loved ones or that he'd die and would never have a chance to be with Will. His head was a jumble of emotions and thoughts, and it never quieted down.

Marcel missed sleep. At least when he'd slept, he'd been able to leave the world behind. Now, the only thing he could do was stretch out on the couch and stare at the ceiling, or alternatively, at the wall. Will had offered to leave the TV on the entire night so Marcel would have something to watch, but Marcel had declined. He didn't want to watch TV. He wanted to go back to his body and his life.

He sighed and stepped back, headed to the living room. He couldn't spend the entire night watching Will sleep. They might be together now, but he doubted Will would be happy to know he stared at him while he slept.

Since he didn't have anything else to do, Marcel decided to try visiting his body again. He didn't know if York would be there, considering how late it was, but even if he wasn't, Marcel could take advantage of the time he spent in his body and gather as many details as he could from the place he was kept in.

He closed his eyes and slowed his breathing. Now that he'd been doing it for a while, it was easy for him to find and slide into his body. It still felt odd, like he was a visitor in his own body, but he dealt with it.

When he opened his eyes, he was alone. He tried rolling his head to look around, but he couldn't. Hopefully, whatever he could see from the position he was in would be enough.

The big mold spot on the wall was growing. That meant that whatever this place was, it was damp and abandoned. That wasn't surprising, especially since Marcel figured other shifters were being kept here along with him. The person who'd taken them needed a large space to keep the shifters together and give his psychics space where they could take life energy without being noticed.

The fact that there were no windows made him wonder. What places didn't have windows and were as big as this room? Probably something industrial, which would explain why it was in such a bad state. If it had been abandoned and was on the outskirts of town, people were probably breaking in and sleeping, at least until the guy behind all of this had taken over. It would give him space, time, and the anonymity he needed to gather the life energy he was seeking.

A movement made Marcel look down. York was coming toward him from a door Marcel hadn't noticed until now. He was biting into a piece of what looked like dry bread, looking as if it was the best thing he'd ever eaten. The bastard stealing Marcel's life energy was starving York, and once Marcel was back in his human form, he'd shift and eat him.

He wasn't angry at York. He had been when he'd realized York was behind this, but now that he'd seen him several times, he could tell York wasn't willingly doing this. What-ever his boss had over him, it was enough to keep York here, stealing Marcel's life energy instead of running away. York was terrified, and Marcel couldn't berate him for that.

If possible, York looked even worse than he had that morn-ing. He stopped next to the bed, and this time, he didn't freak out when he saw Marcel's eyes were open.

"Are you okay?" Marcel asked, worried York might be about to faint.

To his surprise, instead of answering, York started crying. A sob racked through his thin chest, and he wrapped his arms around himself and lowered his head. He couldn't hide the fact that he was crying, though. Marcel could smell it, but even if he hadn't been able to, the way York's shoulders shook made it obvious.

"York?" Marcel asked gently. "What's going on? Can I do anything for you?"

York shook his head, then nodded. When he looked up at Marcel, his eyes were puffy and his cheeks glistened with tears. "Why are you so nice?" he asked.

"Because you need it. I don't know what the guy you're working for has on you, but you're not here willingly. You're being starved, and you're terrified. You need someone to protect you and take care of you."

"And you'll be that person?"

"I can't do much right now, but I'll do as much as I can. That's why I need my body back. When I do, I'll be able to help you."

York shook his head. "Not right away. You'll be weak when you wake up."

"Then my friends will help you."

"Why would they? I hurt you."

"They'll help because I asked them to. And yes, you did hurt me, but you were forced to do it. I don't blame you."

York rubbed his face. "You should. This is all my fault."

"I doubt that's the case, but you don't have to think about that now. The only thing you need to focus on is getting out of here."

"I can't."

"You can do whatever you want, especially with my help."

York glanced around, but the room was quiet apart from them. Still, he moved closer to the bed and took Marcel's hand. Marcel almost jerked back, and he might have if he'd been able to.

York noticed and snatched his hand away. "I wasn't going to take your energy. I swear."

"I know. I'm just a bit wary because I have no idea where my body is or how to get it out of there."

York sat in the chair, but he didn't retake Marcel's hand. Marcel was sorry he'd reacted the way he had, but who could blame him?

"You promise you'll take me with you when you leave?" York asked.

"I do."

"You don't even know what I did."

"It doesn't matter. You're not a bad person. You feel guilty about what's going on and that you wish you weren't a part of it. You were forced into it, right?"

York hesitated. "Not in the beginning. I wanted something, and this guy promised he'd help me. I realized he'd been lying to me, but by then, it was too late. I was stuck here, and I still am."

"What did he promise you?"

York shook his head. "It doesn't matter. I knew I was going to hurt people when I agreed to this, but I still did. I don't deserve to be saved."

"I don't think you should be the one to decide that." Because it was obvious there was more to it than what York was saying. Marcel wanted to ask more questions and find out what it was, but that could wait until later. He and York needed to get out of here first, and they needed to do it as soon as possible.

"And I don't think I deserve to be saved," York murmured. "But I'll help you. You're the only one who asked me if I was okay since I arrived here. You're the only one who cares, even though I don't understand why you do."

"I don't need you to understand. I just need you to accept that I do and help me get both of us out."

Will jerked awake. For a moment, he stayed still, listening and trying to understand why he wasn't asleep anymore. He didn't usually wake in the middle of the night.

Then he saw the figure standing by the foot of his bed.

He scrambled into a sitting position with his back against the headboard and threw his hands forward. If it was a ghost, he'd banish the motherfucker to hell and back.

"It's me," the figure said, raising their hands.

The figure came closer, and Will relaxed. "What the fuck? Were you watching me sleep again?" His heart was racing, but since Marcel was still a spirit, he couldn't hear it the way he would have if he'd been in his body.

"Tempting, but not this time. I talked to York."

The teasing flew right out the window. "What did he say?"

"He told me where my body is."

Will threw himself out of bed, stumbled on the jeans he'd left on the floor last night, snatched them, and pushed one of his legs into it. "I'll call Jerome and the others. What did York say? Where are you?"

Marcel stayed with Will as Will quickly dressed, throwing on the first t-shirt he found in his drawer, even though it was an awful tie-die one with a wolf howling at the moon in the front. Lindsey had found it amusing, and Will wouldn't care if it got ruined by whatever happened tonight.

"We're in the industrial district. He's not allowed out of the warehouse where they're staying, but he knows where it is because of the coffee shop and our date."

Will grabbed his phone and dialed Jerome's number from

memory. He didn't bother looking at the time. He didn't care what time it was, and neither would Jerome.

"Someone had better be dying," Jerome rasped when he answered.

"Not yet, but Marcel might if we don't move now. He knows where his body is."

Jerome sounded awake now. "Where?"

"Industrial district. Call Victor and Timothy. I'll call Leo. See all of you at my place in twenty minutes."

Will hung up before Jerome could say anything. He knew his friend would have demanded answers, and while Will wanted to give them to him, it was better if they were all present for it.

Will called Leo on his way to the kitchen to make a pot of coffee. Once he'd started it, he and Marcel sat down, and Will wrote down the directions York had given Marcel and looked for the place on his phone.

"He said you're in a warehouse?" he asked.

"Yeah. An old meatpacking plant."

Will grimaced. "That doesn't sound like a horror movie at all. Where in the plant are you being kept?"

"He said we were near the old refrigerator cells, where the meat was cut up and packed."

The thought made Will shudder, but he wouldn't hesitate if it meant getting Marcel's body back.

Leo was the first to arrive. He looked around Will's apartment, but he couldn't see Marcel. Will sent him to the kitchen for the coffee, and by the time he was back, Jerome and Lindsey were there, too. Timothy and Victor were the last to arrive. Timothy was jittery as if he'd drunk too many coffees already, but he still took the cup Leo offered.

"I was still awake," he muttered as he took a sip.

"Will you be okay helping us?" Will needed to know he could count on everyone.

"Of course. It's not the first time I've pulled an all-nighter. Besides, you need as many dragons as you can get."

He wasn't wrong. Will hoped that between three psychics and three dragons, they wouldn't have too many problems getting Marcel's body out of the plant, along with York. He was helping them now, and that was all that mattered.

"I called my parents," Jerome said. "Mom and Dad wanted to come, but I convinced them to stay back with Elijah and the rest of the clan. They're ready to step in if we need them, although it would be better if we kept the number of shifted dragons down, just in case. We don't want humans to realize we exist."

Will agreed, but it felt good to know they had an entire dragon clan watching their backs.

He quickly explained what Marcel had told him. Marcel added a few details, but nothing that would change the decision to head there tonight. They'd never be more ready to do this than they were now, and the sooner they got Marcel back, the better it would be. York had told Marcel he had plenty of life energy to spare, but no one wanted to risk it.

"Why is York doing this?" he asked once they'd disbanded and he and Marcel, along with Timothy in the back, were on their way to the plant. Leo, Lindsey, Jerome, and Victor were in Jerome's car, headed the same way.

Marcel sighed. "We talked. He didn't give me many details, but he did say that he wanted something, and this guy promised he'd get it if he helped. York didn't know what he was supposed to do exactly, and once he realized it, there was no going back."

"Why is he stealing your life energy?"

"It's not only mine. Apparently, they've been kidnapping shifters from all over town and even the towns around here. They're channeling it to raise and control the ghosts."

That explained the new ghostly activity in town. "What

for? I mean, ghosts are annoying, but they're ghosts. Most people can't see them."

"Exactly. They can get in and out of places without anyone noticing. If someone could control all the ghosts in town, they could spy on people, steal secrets, blackmail government officials, or anyone else. They could even use ghosts to kill people. You've seen how many people got hurt recently. Imagine the same thing, but with thousands of ghosts."

Will didn't want to think about it. It was horrifying, especially when he realized that the guy behind this would be using ghosts who wouldn't do this normally. He'd force them to hurt the people they'd left behind when they died, and they'd have to obey. Will didn't know if they'd realize what they were doing, but he didn't want to risk it.

"Is this something psychics can do?" Timothy asked from the backseat after Will had explained what Marcel had said.

"I don't know. Why don't you call Victor and put him on speaker? The others need to hear this."

Will focused on the road as Timothy filled everyone else in. He cut in a few times, but he didn't have to explain how bad this news was.

"Can any psychic do this?" Timothy asked Victor when he was done.

"Psychics deal in death," Victor answered. "Most psychics use their gift to help people cross over and protect the living, but yes, we can somewhat control ghosts. We have to be able to do that in order to banish them when necessary. Not every ghost wants to cross over, and some have to be forced."

"But this guy's been controlling dozens of ghosts," Will pointed out.

"One psychic couldn't do this. We don't have enough life energy, not all at once. He might be working with other psychics, but I can't imagine a lot of us would want to help him."

"So he's stealing life energy from shifters."

"Yes." Victor sounded grim. "He could have used humans, but they don't have nearly as much life energy as shifters. And since he can't steal all the life energy he needs on his own, he forced other psychics to do it for him."

So this guy was keeping not only the shifters but also psychics hostage. How many people would they find at the plant? How many of them would they have to fight?

The dragon shifters could take care of the psychics and the guy in charge, but it would come to Lindsey, Victor, and Will to face the ghosts that would undoubtedly be thrown at them.

Will had wanted to find out what he could do as a psychic, and he was about to — in the worst situation possible.

Marcel hated that he wouldn't be able to help. He was the only one who couldn't fight, which meant he'd have to stay back and watch the others put themselves in danger to save him. He'd never felt so powerless, but hopefully, it would be over soon.

Will parked a little away from the plant. They'd agreed that would be better so that no one inside the plant realized they were there, but it might make retreat messy. They'd have to get back to the cars to leave, and it could become a problem if someone was after them. Marcel didn't like any of this, but he realized it was because he was afraid someone he loved would get hurt. He wanted his body back, but not if it meant losing one of his friends.

But there would be no convincing them to go home. The only person Marcel needed here was Victor, and while Marcel didn't know him well, he didn't want to put him in danger, just like he didn't want to put Jerome and Will in danger. Asking any of them to go back would earn him a scowl and possibly some insults, so he didn't even suggest it.

They climbed out of Will's car and met in the darkness.

Marcel was nervous, and he wasn't the only one. Timothy was even more jittery than before, even though he hadn't gotten any more coffee. Will had frowned the entire drive here, and Jerome looked like he was ready to blast through walls to get to Marcel. He probably was.

"What's the plan?" Timothy asked.

"The dragons should shift," Jerome said. "One dragon for each psychic. We don't know what's inside, so it'll be better if we stay in teams. This way, we should be able to cover anything." He looked at Will. "Has Marcel said anything else?"

"Not anything you haven't heard already."

Jerome nodded. His expression was tight but steady, and Marcel knew that whatever happened, his brother would get them out of here. He just hoped to be able to go back to his body when Jerome did.

He looked around. He couldn't see much, but he hadn't expected anything different from what he was seeing. All around them, buildings rose in the darkness. None of them were tall, but they were massive in length.

They were in the industrial district, but in an area where no one worked anymore. All the plants and warehouses had been closed a while back, which had to be why the psychics had chosen this place to steal life energy from shifters. No one would bother them here.

Well, no one but Marcel and the others.

Marcel swallowed. This was it. They were about to get his body back, and once this evening was over, he'd go back to his old life. It would be different, but for the better, not worse.

"I'll go with Lindsey," Jerome said.

"I assume Marcel will stick with Will?" Leo asked.

Will looked at Marcel, who shrugged. "I can stay with you, but I think I should go back to York. He's terrified. Besides, I'm not going to be of any help, even if I stay with you."

Will nodded and turned his attention to Leo. "No. He'll go

to York and stay with the guy and his body."

"Right. Well, I'm still going with you."

Will smiled. "Thank you."

Leo shrugged and looked away. "Marcel would kill me if I allowed anything to happen to you."

"I suppose this leaves me with Timothy," Victor said smoothly.

Timothy's eyes were wide, but he nodded. Marcel wasn't sure it was the best idea to pair the most experienced psychic with the youngest dragon, but he had faith in everyone. If they could, they'd get him out of here. If they couldn't, well, it wouldn't be their fault.

"Where are we going?" Leo asked.

Will looked at his phone and gestured in the direction of one of the buildings. It was only a few minutes away from them, so walking there wouldn't be a problem. "That one. From what Marcel said, I think I know where he is, but I'm not making any promises. I could be wrong."

"What are the odds you are?"

"I don't know. We're going in blind, unfortunately."

Leo nodded. "That's why I'll be with you. You think about finding Marcel. I'll watch your back."

They all looked at each other for a moment. Not all of them could see Marcel, but he could see them, and he wanted to cry at the thought of losing one of these people. He'd give his life if it meant saving them, but none would ever agree to that. They'd been looking for him since he'd been taken, and they'd take it to the end, no matter what happened.

"What will you be doing when we get inside?" Will asked.

"I told you. I'll find York."

"Are you sure we can trust him?"

"As sure as I can be. He's terrified, Will. Whatever he's doing, he's not doing it because he wants to. I promise you that."

Will stared at Marcel for a moment before nodding. "I

believe you. I just hope you're not wrong."

"So do I."

"All right," Jerome said loud enough that everyone in their group heard him. "Dragons, it's time to shift."

Marcel took a step back, wishing he could shift, too. He missed being in his dragon form and flying in the night, just like he missed being in his human form and eating or doing anything else. He wanted to be able to kiss Will and to tell him how much he meant to him. He supposed he could do that, but it wasn't the same, and he didn't want to make promises he might not be able to keep if he ended up dying.

The psychics and Marcel watched as Leo, Timothy, and Jerome undressed and shifted. There wasn't a lot of space in the area for three adult dragons, but thankfully, Timothy was on the smaller side. Still, the sooner they did this, the better it would be.

Jerome and Timothy were both shades of green. Jerome's color was dark, while Timothy was turquoise. Leo, on the other hand, was blue. It would be hard for Timothy to hide, but Marcel supposed it would have been anyway. Dragons were too big to hide, whatever situation they were in.

Timothy stretched his wings, smacking Leo in the face with one of them. Leo growled and swatted Timothy's ass, making him jump. The ground shook under his paws. Marcel rolled his eyes. Trust his friends to play around even when his life was on the line.

"I've seen Jerome and you shift several times, but it still amazes me," Will whispered.

"Once I'm back in my body, I'll take you flying."

Will turned wide eyes to Marcel. "Really?"

"Unless you're afraid of heights?"

Will shook his head. "I'm not. I can't wait for you to take me flying."

Marcel couldn't either. He wouldn't have to wait long.

They were going in, and they were coming out with his body. There could be no other outcome to this.

If there would be, he didn't want to think about it.

Will wished there was more he could do for Marcel. The situation had to be hard for him. He was watching his friends go into danger to save him, and there was nothing he could do to help them. Will knew how frustrated he'd have been in the situation, and he could imagine the same went for Marcel.

"I like that plan," he murmured.

Marcel smiled. "We'll do many things once I'm back in my body."

The first thing Will thought about was that he'd finally get to kiss Marcel. The second was that he wanted to spend the next weekend in bed with Marcel, learning his body and marking him. Everything would be a mess once Marcel was back in his body, but Will didn't care. Even if Marcel decided he didn't want to be with him after all, Will would be happy. Marcel would at least have the opportunity to make that kind of decision, which was all he'd wanted since this started.

Marcel's body was in the building in front of them, unconscious and being sucked dry from life energy. Will would find him, and he'd save him, even if he had to drag his body outside by himself.

He eyed Leo's form. He probably *wouldn't* have to drag Marcel outside, but still. He was ready to do it.

"What else do you want to do once you're back in your body?" he asked, hoping to distract himself from what was about to happen. He'd never been in a fight, especially one so serious. The people inside would do anything to stop him and the others from taking Marcel back, and people could get hurt. People could even die, and that wasn't something Will was used to dealing with.

"I can't wait to drink coffee again. I want to take a walk and feel the wind on my face. I want to fly, and I can't wait to do it with you."

"What else?" Will croaked.

"You know what else," Marcel murmured, leaning closer. "I want to kiss you until you can't breathe. I want to explore your body and find out how much it's changed since we were teenagers."

Will's cheeks felt like they were on fire. He cleared his throat. "You don't know how much it changed. I mean, it's not like you ever touched it when we were kids."

A low grumble made both Marcel and Will look sideways. Jerome lowered his head so he could look Will in the eyes with one of his and arched a brow. Will knew what he was asking without needing to say the words, and he shook his head. Now wasn't the moment to tell Jerome he and Marcel were together. He wasn't even sure that was the case. Sure, it was what Marcel had said he wanted, but that was before. Now, he was getting his body back, and while he sounded like he couldn't wait to get his hands on Will, Will didn't want to keep his hopes up just in case Marcel changed his mind.

"Is everyone ready?" Victor asked, his voice barely louder than a whisper.

Will looked in Jerome's big amber eye and nodded. "We're ready," he confirmed.

"Let's go inside, then. Will, Lindsey, remember what I taught you about ghosts. Don't be afraid of them. Use your gift to make them do what you want."

Will grimaced. "I can't say I'm looking forward to that."

"Neither am I, but in this situation, it's either control them or die. Do you want to risk it?"

"I'll do what I have to do."

Victor nodded curtly. "Good. Let's go in."

Will stuck close to Leo as they moved toward the plant.

They'd already decided who would enter where, and Will hoped the three groups would find their entrance point easily. It was hard to say, considering how long this place had been abandoned and who had taken it over. It was entirely possible that the guy had changed things inside and closed off exits, but Will needed to focus on the good, not on what might happen to make all of this a disaster.

Leo went ahead. Even in the darkness, Will could see the other two dragons moving around the building, and he hoped no one was looking out the window. The dragons quickly flew around the building once, then Leo was back by Will's side. He stayed in his dragon form as Will approached the door he'd chosen to enter. He sucked in a breath, grabbed the handle, and slowly pushed.

It moved.

He huffed in relief and pushed the door open. It made so much noise he was afraid someone had heard him, and he opened it all the way, hiding behind it while Leo took point. He wouldn't be able to go inside in his dragon form, but he didn't need to in order to be dangerous.

Leo poked his head through the door and looked around. It took him a moment, but when he retreated back outside, he nodded at Will and quickly shifted. "As far as I can see, no one's there."

"I'm going to have to trust you on that."

"You'd better. You can't see in the dark the way I can. I'd ask you to stay behind, but I know you wouldn't do it."

"I can't afford to. What if this guy uses the ghosts he controls to attack you? No, we're doing this together, and that's that."

Leo nodded. "You're a good match for Marcel. He's stubborn as hell, too."

Will shook his head. He didn't want to talk about Marcel right now or talk at all. He wanted to find Marcel, get out, and go home.

They snuck in. Marcel went ahead, looking around and making sure no one was hiding in corners or behind doors. Once he was sure the area was empty, he came back. "You can go ahead. I'm going back to York."

"Be careful."

Marcel looked amused. "Shouldn't I be the one to tell you that? Nothing can happen to me, not while I'm a spirit."

"I know. Still, be careful." Will wanted to tell him he didn't trust York and that maybe Marcel shouldn't, either, but he kept the words to himself. Marcel was convinced York was trustworthy, and York had been the one to tell Marcel where his body was. They'd have to trust him, no matter how little Will liked it.

Marcel walked away, and Will watched him until he disappeared from sight. Once Marcel was gone, Will turned his attention to Leo, who was still in his human form. "You should shift again," he said.

Leo nodded but didn't do it right away. "You were talking to Marcel."

"He said he was going to York."

"He really trusts the guy?"

"As far as I can tell. He's usually a good judge of character, and I want to believe he's right and that York truly is doing this because he's been forced to."

"But you can't be sure."

"I can't be sure of anything right now. I'm terrified we'll do something wrong and that Marcel will get hurt."

But they had to forge ahead. It was the only way to find Marcel and the only way to get him home.

CHAPTER NINE

M arcel walked through the plant, looking for York. York had told him how to find the room where his body was kept, but it wasn't easy. He was afraid he'd cross paths with one of the other psychics York had said worked there, because if he did, he wouldn't be able to hide. He was used to people not seeing him, but almost everyone around here would be able to. It could be dangerous, especially if they realized who he was and what he was trying to do.

So even though he was a spirit, Marcel was cautious as he walked down the hallways and turned corners.

The place was a disaster. Marcel had expected that, but seeing it still rankled him. He had a hard time believing so many people were being kept there, both shifters and psychics.

The plant was much bigger than he'd expected it to be. The lights were off, giving it a haunted vibe. Marcel wouldn't have been surprised if it *was* haunted. How many of the other shifters were strong enough to have their spirits walk around trying to find their body? How many of them had been trying to do just that since they'd realized what was happening? Or was Marcel the only one who'd made it?

He didn't want to think that was the case, but he knew that if he hadn't had his friends, he wouldn't be here today. He hoped they'd be able to help every single shifter and psychic, but if they couldn't, they'd still make sure to take the bodies back to their packs. It was the least they could do.

First, they had to find them.

Marcel continued walking down the hallway. He

suspected that if he hadn't been a spirit, he'd be cold. As it was, he couldn't feel anything, but he could hear and see, and he took advantage of that.

The few windows he walked past were broken and looked like they had been for a long time. The floor was concrete in most of the places Marcel walked through. It was cracked, and in some areas closer to the windows, plants had started growing. The dampness had created rot and mold on the walls, so much so that Marcel couldn't imagine anyone living here. It was the perfect place to hide, though, so he wasn't surprised that the guy who was behind all of this had chosen this place.

Marcel finally noticed a light at the end of the hallway he was walking down. The door facing him was cracked just a bit, but it was enough for the light to come through. He hurried toward it, passed through the door, and found himself in the room he'd seen every time he'd visited his body.

It was long but not wide. From his position, Marcel could see more than he had been able to when he'd been in bed, and the sight horrified him.

The bed closest to the entrance was his. He could see his body, stretched out on his back, and York sitting in the chair by it. He was holding Marcel's hand, but Marcel knew he wasn't taking the life energy from him. He'd explained he was going to act as if he were, just in case the guy keeping him there checked on him. The man didn't check often, because apparently he disliked the place, which was fucking ironic. It was still something they had to be careful about, and York's idea was good.

Next to Marcel's bed was a partition like the ones used in hospitals. It was missing the wheels on one side, so it stood crooked, but it did its job of blocking the sight between Marcel and the guy in the bed next to his. The guy was alone, asleep like Marcel's body, and covered up to his chest with a thin sheet. The heart monitor next to the bed told Marcel he was still alive, even though he didn't look like he was. He was incredibly pale, and he looked so fragile that Marcel was afraid he'd break him if he touched him. Marcel supposed it was one of the effects of having his life energy taken, and he could only hope the guy would heal.

Beyond the bed was another partition, then another bed. It continued that way until the end of the room, and Marcel counted seven beds, all of them occupied.

He swallowed. Until now, his focus had been on saving himself and York. Now, he knew he couldn't abandon the people in the beds next to his or in other rooms. He doubted anyone in their little group would be happy once they found out what Marcel wanted to do, but they'd agree. They wouldn't want to leave anyone behind.

Marcel couldn't do anything right now, so he hurried to York's side. York's eyes were closed when Marcel reached him, and Marcel hesitated. Should he slide into his body and talk to York that way? Or should he talk to him as a spirit? York would see him either way, and maybe it was easier for him to stay around as a spirit, at least for now.

"York?" he whispered.

York jerked and looked around with wide eyes. His gaze stopped on Marcel, and he scrambled out of his chair, letting go of Marcel's hand. "You're here," he breathed out.

Marcel nodded. "Thanks to you. I told you I'd come back."

York looked around. "I didn't think you actually would. Are you alone?"

"No. My friends are in the building, too. They'll be here soon."

The door through which Marcel had entered slammed against the wall. York paled so much Marcel was afraid he might faint, and he was relieved when York sat in the chair again. He looked back, wanting to see what was happening, and saw a man walking in through the door. Since York was close to the door, the guy paused and looked at him. "Why aren't you working?" he snapped.

"I am. I just took a break for a moment, but I'm going back to it."

"You better. You know what will happen if you don't."

"I—please. I promise I'm not doing anything, just resting. I'm hungry."

Marcel knew from the guy's expression he wasn't going to like what happened next. The guy strode toward York, who tried to make himself smaller on the chair, curling around his chest and knees. It wasn't enough to stop the guy, though. He grabbed York's arm and pulled him out of the chair, jerking him around as if York were nothing more than a doll.

"You'll get food once you're done with your work. Are you complaining?"

York shook his head. "I promise I'm not, Kurt."

Kurt raised his hand and backhanded York. Marcel didn't think Kurt was a psychic, since he hadn't even looked at him, but he wished he could do more. He wanted to help York, but he didn't know how.

He looked around, frantic to stop Kurt from hitting York again. There wasn't much in the room, so he grabbed the chair York had been sitting in and raised it, even though it shouldn't have been possible. Kurt never saw it coming. Marcel hit him on the back, but unfortunately, it wasn't enough to get Kurt to his knees.

Kurt released York and looked around. "Who did that?" he asked.

York shook his head. "I don't know."

Kurt turned his attention back to York. "You're lying. It was a ghost."

"But I didn't recognize him."

Kurt hit York again. York fell to the ground and scrambled

until his back was against the foot of Marcel's bed. Kurt took a step forward, maybe to hit him again, but he stopped.

York's lower lip was split and blood was seeping from it. His eye was reddened, and Marcel suspected it would turn black soon and maybe swell.

"After everything I did for you, you're working against me?" Kurt asked.

He moved toward York again. York whimpered and wrapped his arms around his head, trying to protect himself.

It didn't help.

Kurt kicked York in the side, making him cry out. He didn't attempt to get away, though, and Marcel knew it was a sign that this wasn't the first time Kurt had beat him. There was nowhere for York to run, so instead, he was staying and pushing through this as well as he could, protecting his head while Kurt beat the rest of his body.

Marcel was enraged. He grabbed the chair again, but he was tired. He'd never done much as a spirit except trying to get to his body, and he was feeling it. He should have trained more, but it was too late for that.

It was too late for a lot of things. Marcel managed to hit Kurt again, but it was the last thing he did. When Kurt turned toward him, Marcel dropped the chair and tried to breathe. Darkness closed around him, and he couldn't resist its pull. He'd done too much, and now, he was going to pay the price.

He just hoped York wouldn't get hurt more than he already had.

There were hospital beds everywhere Will looked. Every single one of them was occupied, and while most of the people in them were alive, some had sheets pulled over their faces.

Will didn't know what to say. He wasn't sure there was anything he *could* say at all.

"How many people do you think are here?" he asked Leo.

The dragon shifter had shifted back to his human form because he couldn't walk down the hallways as a dragon, but Will knew he was ready to shift back at any second. Will was grateful they were able to talk. He felt less alone, even though it was awkward not to stare at Leo's naked body.

"Impossible to say," Leo murmured.

Because it wasn't the first room they'd walked in that was set up this way. It was the third, and both the first and the second rooms were as full as this one. They also still hadn't found Marcel's body, which meant there were more rooms. There had to be at least thirty people here, if not more, and all of them were shifters someone was stealing life energy from.

Will took a step forward. Some of the beds had people sitting next to them, holding the hands of the people in the bed. Will knew it meant they were stealing life energy, which was good, because he was able to walk behind them without catching their attention. He and Leo tiptoed out of the room, entering the one next to it.

The situation didn't change. There were still people stuck in the beds, with other people sucking life energy from them. This time, though, someone noticed them. A woman was getting up from the chair next to a shifter's bed, and she looked back just as Will stepped into the room. She was blonde with blue eyes, her skin pale as if she hadn't seen the sun in a long time. Her eyes were wide, and before Will could say anything, she opened her mouth and screamed.

Will and Leo looked at each other.

"I need to shift. I might hurt some of the people in the beds, but I think it's the only way to do this."

Will didn't like the thought of hurting anyone, but he nodded. It wouldn't help any of the shifters in those beds if he and Leo got hurt.

Leo shifted as a small group of people rushed into the

room. From the way they were dressed, Will suspected they were guards. He was relieved more than ever to have Leo with him, because it meant he didn't have to fight. Leo breathed a small flame, burning one guy so quickly he didn't even get to scream.

Will looked around. The woman who'd first screamed was still there, staring at him. He ran toward her, wanting to help her, but he realized he shouldn't have been worried when she turned around and ran away. She was still screaming, calling for a guy called Kurt, and Will had the suspicion he was the guy York had been talking about.

She barged into the room next to this one. Will went after her and regretted it as soon as he walked in.

The woman had thrown herself into a guy's arms, and from the looks of things, the guy had been beating someone up. A small figure was huddled at the foot of the bed, and Will's stomach sank when he realized the guy had to be York, because the man in the bed behind him was Marcel.

Marcel's spirit was nowhere to be seen. Will didn't have time to stop and wonder what that meant. Kurt pushed the woman away, and Will heard the sound of his clothes tearing. He was shifting, which meant Will was in trouble.

"Leo?" he called out, never looking away from Kurt.

The sound of footsteps behind him made him turn around. He relaxed when he saw it was Leo, in his human form again, and he gestured at Kurt. "He's a shifter," he said.

Leo nodded and shifted. His dragon form was too big for the room, and he stood hunched. He couldn't move easily, which hopefully wouldn't be too much of a problem, because Kurt was done shifting.

Will had never seen anything like him. He was used to dragons, and he didn't know any other shifters, not that he was aware of. Kurt looked a bit like a dragon, with scaly skin, spikes running down his body to the tip of his tail, and wings.

His face was different, though. Instead of a snout like Leo, he had a beak, and when he opened his mouth, a long, forked tongue slithered out. He cried out, the sound high-pitched and sounding a bit like a chicken.

Kurt's shifted form was smaller than Leo's. Will waited for him to attack, but just then, the door behind them slammed open, and another dragon tried to push through. He couldn't because the door was so small, but he pushed his head through it and spat fire at Kurt.

Jerome was pissed, and he obviously had every intention of taking it out on Kurt.

Kurt cried out again, but instead of attacking like Will expected him to, he turned around and ran for the other door.

"He's running away," Lindsey cried out.

Will had no intention of going after Kurt. It wouldn't end well for him if he reached the guy, and he knew his limits. If Leo and Jerome wanted to go, he wouldn't try to stop them. He had something else to focus on.

The woman was still standing there, and Will hoped Lindsey would keep an eye on her. He ignored her and crouched next to York, but when he reached for the man, York winced and shied away from him. Will raised his hands, wanting to show York he didn't mean any harm.

"Are you York?" he asked, just to be sure.

York cracked his eyes open and looked at him. "Who are you?"

"My name is Will. I'm Marcel's boyfriend."

York licked his lips. He winced when his tongue scraped against the blood on his lower lip, but he didn't say anything about it. "You're here to save him?" he asked instead.

Will nodded. "I am." He got to his feet. "Can you help? Where's his spirit? Why isn't he waking up?"

Will didn't know what to do. Victor had warned them he'd need to do something specific to get Marcel's spirit back into his body, but it was too advanced for Will to know how to do it. He'd have to wait until Victor got there, but he didn't know if they had that kind of time.

He stepped closer to the bed. Marcel looked like he remembered, yet at the same time, he was nothing like it. His body appeared smaller in the hospital bed, half-covered by a white sheet. He was paler than Will had ever seen him, almost as if he were fading.

Will swallowed. "Is it too late?" The heart monitor told him Marcel was still alive, but it didn't mean they weren't too late.

York joined him. "It's not. It'll be okay once he has a bit of time to recuperate. I stopped pulling life energy from him in the past few hours."

"Why isn't he waking up, then?"

"Because Kurt had his girlfriend put a spell on him and every other shifter here. He didn't want to risk them waking up."

"Can she take the spell off?"

York looked back, and when Will did the same, he saw that the woman wasn't there anymore.

"She's gone," York whispered.

"*She* was Kurt's girlfriend?"

York nodded. "She was, and I don't know how to take the spell off. I'm just a psychic, but she was both a psychic and a witch. I'm sorry."

Will stared at Marcel's body. Had they arrived too late?

CHAPTER TEN

For a while, it felt like Marcel was floating. He didn't know what it meant, but it wasn't uncomfortable, so he was happy to stay where he was.

He didn't know how long it lasted, but after a bit, he started to feel achy, as if he'd trained too hard for too long and his body was rebelling. He groaned and tried to move, but he couldn't, not without pain flaring.

That got his attention. If he was a spirit, he wouldn't be feeling pain.

He opened his eyes and tried to sit up. A hand pressed against his chest and pushed him back down, and he struggled against it, needing to get out of here. Where was York? And Kurt? What was happening?"

"Stop panicking," a voice said.

It took Marcel a moment to recognize it as Will's, but once he did, he stopped struggling. Will would protect him. He'd tell him if something was wrong and Marcel needed to defend himself.

Marcel sucked in a breath and lowered himself back to his pillow. He blinked, trying to see Will but unable to, at least until Will moved and Marcel saw his face hovering just above his.

"Will?" Marcel croaked.

Will moved away. Marcel wanted to tell him to come back, but he waited, knowing Will wasn't abandoning him. When he appeared again, he was holding a plastic cup Marcel could only hope was filled with water. A straw poked from it, and

Will settled it between Marcel's lips.

"Drink, but not too much. Victor said it's going to take a while for your body to heal and settle down now that you're back in it."

Marcel obeyed, flopping back against the pillow once he was done. Even drinking felt like it had been too much for him. He was exhausted.

"What happened?" he asked, his voice clearer now. "Am I back in my body?"

Will put down the cup, and Marcel felt him take one of his hands. "You are. Welcome home, Marcel."

Marcel's eyes burned. He didn't want to cry, but he was overwhelmed. "What happened? Is everyone safe?"

"Victor got hurt, but he's okay."

"Tell me everything," Marcel begged.

"Victor said not to, but I know you. You won't be able to rest until you know."

Marcel was glad Will understood that.

Will sat on the edge of the mattress by Marcel's hip without releasing his hand, and Marcel latched on to that feeling. Will's hand was warm and dry, and when he linked their fingers together, Marcel knew he would never let go.

He didn't want him to.

"What do you remember?" Will asked.

"Finding York. A guy came in and started beating him up."

Will nodded. "That's what Leo and I walked in on. We found a woman taking life energy from a shifter in the room next to yours. When she saw us, she ran away screaming. Apparently, she was Kurt's girlfriend."

"Kurt?" Marcel had heard the name, but he couldn't place it at the moment.

"The shifter who took you and every other shifter in that room. The guy who was using ghosts through his girlfriend."

"Tell me everything."

"Kurt was the one who kidnapped you and the other shifters, along with York and other psychics. His girlfriend was one of them, but she and York weren't the only ones working for Kurt. Most of those people were there because Kurt forced them to, but not all. Some were there because they truly believed in what Kurt was doing, and we had to fight our way to you. Well, the others did. Leo and I were lucky, and we managed to get to you without too many problems."

"Why were they doing this?"

"I can only tell you what York explained, but apparently, Kurt had the intention of raising an army of ghosts."

"Didn't you say he was a shifter?"

"He is. I didn't know what it was when I first saw it, but Timothy explained when I described it to him. Apparently, Kurt is a cockatrice shifter."

Marcel blinked. It had been a while since he'd heard those words. Cockatrices were even rarer than dragon shifters, and that was saying something. "What was he planning to do with his army of ghosts?"

Will shrugged. "Your guess is as good as mine. From what York was able to tell us, Kurt resents having to hide. He wants an army of ghosts and fighters, but to fight against what, I don't know."

"He ran away?"

Will nodded. "He's not the only one. His girlfriend disappeared, too, along with a few other psychics. Those who stayed were being forced into this."

Marcel wasn't surprised. "How's York?"

"He'll be fine. He's banged up, and he needs food and rest, but at the end of this, he should be okay."

"What about Victor? You said he was hurt?" Marcel's eyes were starting to close, but he couldn't allow himself to fall asleep before he knew everyone was okay.

"He crossed paths with Kurt as Kurt escaped. He was

scratched on the arm, but he'll be fine. I also called your parents and the clan. They were waiting outside the plant like we'd asked them to, and they stepped in to take care of the shifters we found with you."

Marcel swallowed. "How many?"

Will sighed and squeezed Marcel's hand. "Thirty-three. We found five of them dead, and the others are in bad shape, like you. Victor, Lindsey, and I are working to reunite their spirits with their bodies, but it's not easy. Not all of them were anchored the way you were. Some of the spirits aren't coming back, and we don't know how to find them."

Marcel closed his eyes. He realized he'd been lucky, and he'd known not everyone would be. It was still sad to learn that some of the shifters had lost their spirits and that their bodies wouldn't be waking up.

"But we're not giving up," Will added. "For now, their bodies are with the clan, and the clan will take care of them. The psychics are with them, too."

"Even York?"

Will shook his head. "He wanted to stay close to you. He wants to talk to you, but I wasn't sure you'd be up for it."

"I'm tired."

Will leaned down and kissed Marcel's forehead. "Then you should sleep. Everything else can wait."

"Don't leave me," Marcel said, clinging onto Will's hand.

"I'm not going anywhere. Even if I'm not here when you open your eyes, I won't be far. I promise."

Marcel forced himself to release Will's hand. He trusted him and believed his words, which meant that the next time he woke up, Will *would* be right there with him.

That was the only thing that allowed Marcel to let go and give in to sleep. He had to get some rest if he wanted to get out of here—wherever *here* was—as soon as possible. He could finish healing and resting once he was home. After spending so much time in a hospital bed, he wanted out of the bed he was in now, and as soon as possible. Will and Jerome wouldn't allow him to leave until they were sure he was up to it, though, and that meant sleep and healing.

Hopefully, the next time he woke up, he'd feel better. Even if he didn't, he wasn't in danger anymore. Will had rescued him, just like he'd promised he would.

It wasn't easy to convince everyone to leave Marcel's room. Marcel's parents had been there since he'd arrived, as had Jerome and everyone else. They all wanted to be present when he next woke up, but Will could imagine how overwhelming it would be. Besides, some of them hadn't slept since they'd brought Marcel back, and that had been a day and a half ago.

When it came to that, Will probably shouldn't be talking. He'd only slept a few hours in the chair next to Marcel's bed, and he felt like he could sleep an entire week, but he wasn't about to try. He needed Marcel to be awake again first and to make sure Marcel truly was okay.

That was all Will asked for. He knew it would take time for Marcel to get over what had happened, but he wanted Marcel to be okay. Physically, he'd been healing fast, thanks to being a dragon shifter. The clan had also made sure one of their healers helped, and she took her job very seriously, dumping potions and whatnot down Marcel's throat when he was only a little awake.

Will was still worried.

He'd just convinced Marcel's parents and his brother to go home and get some rest, or at the very least, to go downstairs and grab coffee and food. He was pretty sure Marcel's parents had finally gone home, but Jerome wasn't going anywhere. He and the others had vanished, though. Will flopped into the chair that had become his, considering how much time he'd spent in it. He was pretty sure the imprint of his ass would never fade from it.

They couldn't take Marcel to a hospital, so instead, they'd done the next best thing and had brought him to the clan. Will didn't fully understand why Marcel and Jerome weren't part of the clan while their parents were, but he didn't think it mattered. The alpha had welcomed them, given them a guest room, and called the healer. He'd been putting up with their little group since they'd arrived with patience and a smile, something not many people would have done considering how snarky and grumpy Jerome was. Elijah seemed to understand, and he'd mostly left them alone except for making sure they had as much food as they needed. He'd even offered them the use of some of his guest rooms, and while Victor, Timothy, and Lindsey had accepted the offer, Leo, Jerome, and Will had stuck by Marcel's side.

A grunt from the bed made Will look up. Marcel's eyes were fluttering, and Will scrambled to his feet, eager for Marcel to wake up again. He'd been reassured the first time that happened, and he'd known Marcel would need rest, but he couldn't wait to speak to him.

He didn't want to push, so he hovered there, watching one of his best friends and the man he'd fallen in love with open his eyes. He was so relieved his knees buckled, and he clung to the side of the bed, smiling down at Marcel.

"Hey, sleeping beauty," he murmured.

Marcel blinked. "Will?" he croaked.

Will took one of Marcel's hands. "It's me. How are you feeling?"

"Like I spent the past week running a marathon."

The healer had said Marcel would feel exhausted for days, if not longer. His body needed to replenish the life energy that had been stolen from him, and until then, he'd need a lot of rest. Physically, his body was fine. It was drained of energy, but Marcel's life wasn't in danger.

Will smiled. "It's normal, so don't worry."

Marcel snorted. "I don't think it's possible for me not to worry." He licked his lips. "Is there any water?"

Will pushed away from the bed and grabbed the plastic cup with a straw he'd been keeping on the nightstand for when Marcel woke up again. "Here."

Marcel drank, and even that seemed to exhaust him. When he was done, he flopped back against the pillow and closed his eyes for a moment, but it didn't last long. "What happened? Is everyone okay? Did you tell me Victor had gotten hurt?"

"He did, but it's just a scratch, and the healer already helped him."

"Where are we? Because this doesn't look anything like a hospital."

"That's because it's not. We brought you to the house of the dragon clan alpha."

"Why would you do that?"

"Because Elijah offered, and we couldn't take you to the hospital. How are you feeling, beyond exhausted?"

"Well, I guess. It's a bit strange to be in my body, but I suppose that after weeks of being a spirit, I'll have to get used to it again. How are you? How's everyone else?" He looked around. "Where are they?"

"I just managed to convince your parents to go get some rest. As for the others, they're all here."

"And how long have we been here?"

"A day and a half, more or less."

Marcel grimaced and pushed the sheet away from his body. Will grabbed it to pull it back up, but Marcel shook his head. "No. I want to see them."

"You need rest. The healer was clear about that."

"And as grateful as I am to the healer and Elijah, I want to do that at home, where I feel safe and like I belong. Please."

"You shouldn't get up."

Marcel looked Will straight in the eyes. "Please. Take me to your apartment."

Will couldn't say no to that. He didn't really want to, anyway. He'd have taken Marcel straight to his apartment after they found him, but he'd known Marcel needed medical assistance. The healer had said there was nothing else she could do, though. She'd left a stack of bottles containing the same potions she'd given Marcel when she'd first seen him, and Will had strict instruction to give them to him every six hours. He'd feel more comfortable at home, so Will wasn't going to say no.

"You realize your brother is going to try to get you to stay, right?" he asked.

Marcel snorted. "He can try."

"Oh, he will." But that didn't stop him from getting Marcel dressed and to his feet.

Marcel swayed, but Will was there, taking his hand and holding him up. He pulled Marcel against his side and wrapped his arm around his shoulders, ready to help in any way he could. He wasn't surprised Marcel leaned against him. What did surprise him was when Marcel kissed his cheek.

They'd never kissed, not beyond a few kisses on the forehead Will had given Marcel when he'd been unconscious. They'd wanted to, but with Marcel being a spirit, it hadn't been possible. Here and now wasn't the right moment to do it, but they didn't have to make out to feel close to each other, as Marcel had just shown. Since he didn't seem to have a problem with physical affection, Will kissed Marcel's forehead, happy to be able to do at least this.

"Let's go," Marcel said.

"I'll take you home."

"As soon as I've talked to York."

Will glared at Marcel. "I should have known it wouldn't be easy."

"I just want to make sure he's okay."

Will sighed. Marcel cared about York, and Will didn't blame him. They hadn't gotten the entire story out of the psychic yet, but he supposed they were about to.

"He's staying in a guest room," he said as they slowly walked to the door.

"How is he?"

"Well, the healer saw him, too. He'll be okay, but he was starved, and he's exhausted."

"Has Jerome given him grief?"

"He's mostly been glaring at him from the other side of the room. Lindsey made sure he didn't say anything to him."

"That's good."

They finally reached the door. Will opened it, and they shuffled through. Will already knew what was waiting for them outside, and he wasn't surprised when Jerome popped up in front of them seconds after they left the bedroom.

"What are you doing up?"

Marcel smiled. "Hello to you, too."

Jerome glared at his brother, then grabbed him and pulled him into his arms. Will let him go, knowing Jerome would hold Marcel up. He didn't want to relinquish his hold on Marcel, but he wasn't the only person in Marcel's life who'd been worried about him.

"Never do this to me again," Jerome muttered.

"I'll do my best not to get kidnapped a second time," Marcel promised.

Everyone else was there, too, and they all took their turn hugging Marcel and telling him how happy they were he was okay. Even Victor did so, and while Marcel looked nonplussed, he accepted the hug with a smile.

The round of hugging seemed to have exhausted him, though, and when he was finally done, he leaned against Will. Will held him up, more than happy to do so.

"I want to see York," Marcel declared.

Will steeled himself for a fight because he knew Jerome wouldn't be happy.

Marcel wasn't surprised his brother's first reaction was to say no.

"You don't need to see him right now," Jerome said, his tone uncompromising.

"Maybe not, but I *want* to see him."

"After what he did to you?"

"He didn't do anything he wanted to do."

"I'm still not sure about that."

Marcel glared. "I want to talk to him, and that's that. Stop being an asshole. I know what I'm doing, and I won't let you stop me."

Jerome opened his mouth, no doubt to tell Marcel he wouldn't stand for this or something like that, but thankfully, Lindsey stepped in.

He put a hand on Jerome's arm and leaned closer. "Let your brother see York," he said. "He has a right to do it, considering what York did to him. Besides, York isn't dangerous."

Jerome crossed his arms over his chest. "I'm still not a hundred percent convinced he wasn't okay with stealing the life energy."

"It's your right not to believe him, just like it's Marcel's right to believe him and want to see him. Your brother hasn't had the opportunity to make his own choices since he was cast out of his body. Don't do that to him, too."

Jerome's expression turned to horror. "That's not what I

was doing," he told Marcel.

"I know." Marcel stepped forward to hug his brother again. He was grateful to have Will next to him, steadying him as he stepped into Jerome's arms. "I know you were worried, and I promise that even if I die, I'll stick around as a ghost to bother you."

Jerome chuckled and hugged Marcel tightly. "You always were an annoying older brother."

"But you love me anyway."

"Damn right I do." Jerome sighed and stepped back. "Fine. I can't exactly stop you from seeing York."

He could if he really wanted to, but Marcel was relieved his brother wouldn't try.

Their group slowly made its way down the hallway. It was a bit odd to be surrounded by so many people, but it was as if they all wanted to reassure themselves that he truly was okay. He supposed he'd have done the same thing if one of them had been in his situation, and he was happy to see that so many people loved him and wanted him to be okay.

Jerome stopped in front of a closed door. "He's in there. He's been spending most of his time hiding in the bedroom."

"Can you blame him? After what he did, I understand he doesn't want to face you lot." Especially Jerome. Marcel was ready to bet he'd been growling at York since they'd taken him away from Kurt.

"Do you want us to come inside with you?"

"Has York told you what happened to him?"

Jerome shook his head. "He hasn't talked to anyone. Elijah hasn't pushed, but he's going to eventually. He can't exactly allow York to stay with the clan if he can't trust him."

"We'll see what York says." Marcel raised a hand and knocked on the door. He could hear York moving inside, stopping behind the door and listening. "York?" he said. "It's Marcel."

The sound of the door unlocking told Marcel that York was willing to talk to him. The door opened, and York peered out, his eyes wide in his too-thin face.

"You're awake," York whispered.

Marcel smiled at him. "Awake and moving around, yes. Can I talk to you?"

York looked at the group standing behind Marcel. "I suppose all of you want to hear what I have to say?"

He sounded scared, but also like he was pushing through it. Marcel didn't want him to be afraid, but he supposed it would take a while for York to wrap his mind around the fact that no one here would hurt him, not the way Kurt had.

York sighed and stepped aside. "Come in."

They filed into the bedroom. Thankfully, it was wide enough to welcome all of them, although they struggled to find enough places to sit down. Marcel ended up in one of the two armchairs under the window, with Will sitting on the floor next to him. Marcel sighed in relief that he was sitting down. He wasn't sure his legs would have held up for much longer.

He felt like he'd been sick for a long time and was just now healing. He supposed that was true, but he didn't like it. He wanted to go back to his old life, but he didn't think he ever would. It had changed, just like he had.

York closed the door and rubbed his palms on his thighs. "What do you want to know?"

"What happened to you?" Marcel asked.

York sighed and went to sit on the edge of the mattress. "First, I want to apologize for what I did to you."

Marcel shook his head. "Don't worry about it. I know you didn't want to do it and that you were forced into it."

"I was, but it doesn't make it right."

"It doesn't, but I won't hold it against you. I don't hold grudges."

"And I'm grateful for that." York cleared his throat. He looked away from Marcel as if he couldn't find the strength to face him as he explained what had happened to him. "I lost my parents when I was ten. My aunt took in my brother and me, but she had her own kids, and she never really had time for us. It was just Cooper and me against the world for years, and it still should be."

York swallowed heavily. Marcel was pretty sure that even the non-shifters in the room could hear it.

"He died two years ago," York added, his voice barely more than a whisper. "It was a hit and run, and no one paid for what happened. Cooper was only twenty-three."

"I'm sorry for your loss," Marcel murmured. He could barely imagine what his life would be like if he'd lost Jerome when both of them were so young, especially after losing their parents, too.

York's smile was tremulous. "Thank you. When he died, I was lost. He'd been my rock my entire life, and he's not here anymore. Both of us were psychics, but we never had any training. Even so, I decided that I wanted to bring him back. I didn't know how to do it, or even if it was at all possible, but I wasn't going to give up. That's when I met Kurt."

York didn't continue, and Marcel gave him a moment to gather his thoughts. Now that he knew York's history, he understood better why he'd done what he'd done. Marcel couldn't say if he'd try to bring Jerome back if he died, but he understood why York had wanted to.

"Kurt isn't a psychic, but his girlfriend is. They made a lot of promises, and they told me they'd help me bring Cooper back. I shouldn't have trusted them," York continued.

Marcel wanted to reach for him, but, to his surprise, Leo got there before him. He gently touched York's arm, and York looked startled to see him there. He smiled at Leo, and Marcel expected him to have had enough of this conversation.

146

Instead, he continued talking.

"They never explained why they were stealing the life energy of so many shifters, but I knew it couldn't be good. I tried running away once, and Kurt beat me up so badly that I wasn't able to work for a week. I never tried again after that. I still had hope I'd get my brother back, even though I knew this wasn't the right way to do it." He looked at Marcel. "I'm sorry."

"I know," Marcel told him. "And I don't blame you for any of this. I would have done the same if my brother had been the one who'd died. You don't need to apologize anymore. I forgive you."

Besides, Marcel was okay now. Will had told him that not all of the shifters who'd been there had made it out alive, but Marcel had. He supposed it was easy for him to forgive York, but York needed it, and Marcel suspected he did, too. He wanted to leave all of this behind, and the only way to do that was to forgive York.

York was the only one who deserved forgiving, though. If Marcel saw Kurt again, he'd make sure the man could never hurt anyone else.

Will's heart ached for York. It was too easy for him to imagine losing his brother, and he understood why York had wanted to get him back by any means necessary. It didn't make what he'd done right, but it explained it, and Will couldn't find it in himself to be angry or resentful. He looked at Marcel. The dragon shifter was exhausted, but he wasn't moving from the armchair. It looked like Will would have to make some decisions for him, after all.

He waited until York was done talking to intervene. "Marcel needs rest," he declared.

"I'm not going back to the guest room," Marcel protested.

"That's fine. You can come home with Lindsey and me," Jerome intervened.

"Or with me," Leo said.

Jerome and Leo glared at each other. They were being ridiculous, fighting over Marcel as if he were a toy, but Will could understand it.

"I want to go to Will's apartment," Marcel said.

"Why would you want to go there?" Jerome sounded confused.

"Because I know how it is to stay with you and Lindsey, remember?"

That got everyone but York laughing.

"What if we promise to keep our hands to ourselves?"

Marcel shook his head. "I'll be fine with Will. His place has become a home away from home, and I wouldn't mind spending the next week sleeping on his couch."

Both he and Will knew there was no way he was sleeping on the couch, but Will didn't say anything about it. Everyone there except maybe York knew they were together. They'd understand why Marcel wanted some time alone with Will.

It took too long for Will to be able to take Marcel home. His parents were back by the time Marcel was ready to leave, and Marcel had to go through another round of hugging and people worrying over him. His parents insisted on taking him to their home, but Marcel held strong, and Will was grateful. He wanted to have Marcel close and to be able to reassure himself that Marcel was okay. They'd fallen in love while Marcel was a spirit, but what was between them felt different now that he was in his body again. Will didn't know if they could make things work, but he wanted to try. More importantly, he wanted to hold Marcel as he slept and have the proof that Marcel was okay in front of him the entire time.

By the time they managed to extricate themselves from Marcel's family, Marcel was so exhausted he looked like he was about to drop. Will helped him into the car, not surprised when he fell asleep as soon as he drove away from Elijah's house. He let him sleep, knowing he needed it.

Will woke him up as gently as he could when they reached his apartment building. He had to half carry Marcel to the elevator, and they leaned against each other, propping themselves up. Now that Will knew Marcel was okay, he could feel the exhaustion pulling him under. He hadn't gone through what Marcel had, but it didn't mean he wasn't tired.

They stumbled through the door of his apartment. Since Will didn't want Marcel to fall on his face, he closed the door and quickly led him to the bedroom. He helped him take his shoes off and undress, keeping his focus above Marcel's waist as he helped him in the shower. Marcel was exhausted, but he'd been adamant that he wanted to wash.

Will could understand that. He'd showered while Marcel was sleeping off the spells, but Marcel had still been stuck in bed.

Will took advantage of the time Marcel spent in the shower to put together a sandwich for him. It wasn't much, but the healer had warned Marcel to go slow with eating since he hadn't in a while. The spell on Marcel had kept him alive, but his stomach was still empty.

Back in the bedroom, he put the sandwich on the nightstand and helped Marcel out of the shower and into a fresh pair of underwear, then led him to the bed, where he hovered close as Marcel slowly ate half of the sandwich before giving up. Marcel slid deeper under the blankets, and Will tucked them around him. Once he was sure Marcel was fine, he got to his feet, but Marcel grabbed his wrist. "Stay with me?" he slurred.

"I'll come back. I need to check on Cleo."

Marcel nodded. "Don't be too long."

Will was as fast as he could, but he wasn't surprised to find

Marcel asleep by the time he was back in the bedroom five minutes later. He'd made sure Cleo had enough food and water, checked the litter box, and cuddled her for a moment, since he'd been gone for a couple of days. She was more than happy on the couch, and he hoped she'd stay there for the rest of the day.

He undressed as quickly as he could and slid under the sheets, keeping to his side of the bed. He and Marcel hadn't talked about their relationship yet, and he didn't want to invade Marcel's personal space.

He shouldn't have worried. Marcel reached out, his eyes still closed, and hooked an arm around Will's waist. He pulled Will closer, and Will went without protesting. Why should he? He was more than happy to be in Marcel's arms, especially knowing Marcel would be there when he woke up tomorrow.

That was what he had needed to remember. Part of him was terrified that when he'd open his eyes, Marcel would be gone, or that he'd be a spirit again. He wouldn't, but even if something like this happened again, Will and the others would make sure Marcel found his way home.

And right now, Marcel's home was in Will's arms.

CHAPTER ELEVEN

When Marcel opened his eyes, he still couldn't believe he really was here, in Will's bed, and that he could touch Will if he wanted to.

And he did.

Marcel still felt slightly confused and awkward about being back in his body, but it was nothing he couldn't deal with. He didn't care how long it took him to get used to his body again. He was with Will, really this time, and he would take advantage of it.

He turned to his side to look at the man who'd supported him this entire time. Will was still asleep, his lashes casting dark shadows under his eyes. His chest was bare, and the sheet twined around his waist and one leg, leaving the other exposed. His skin was covered in dark hair, and Marcel knew it would feel soft yet prickly if he touched it.

And he could. His hand wouldn't pass through Will like it would have before. The thought of that happening was almost enough to keep Marcel from reaching for Will, but he wouldn't let it. He'd almost lost all of this. He would have if he hadn't found his body and been reunited with it, but he had, and he never wanted to think about what he'd gone through again.

It would have been easy for Will to stay away from Marcel, but he hadn't. He'd stayed by his side the entire time. He'd been there for him when Marcel felt he wouldn't get out of this, and Marcel would never forget it. He'd fallen in love with Will's strength and his soothing presence, and now he wanted to fall in love with the rest of him.

He couldn't wait. He couldn't believe he'd have the opportunity to share a life with Will. What happened beyond them, with Kurt and the ghosts, didn't matter now, and it never would, not when Will was in Marcel's life and by his side.

"You're watching me sleep," Will murmured.

Marcel laughed. "How do you know?"

Will's eyes blinked open. "It's not the first time you've done it."

"It's not." It would be no use denying it. "I'm sorry."

"Don't be." Will leaned forward and kissed Marcel on the corner of his lips. "I don't mind."

"You don't think it makes me a creep?"

"No. I think you needed to feel close to someone when you weren't in your body and that you found it helpful."

"I'm in my body now."

"But are you used to it again?" Will rolled to face Marcel fully. "We haven't talked about it yet, but I can imagine it's not easy for you to wrap your mind around the fact that everything is back to normal. You spent weeks as a spirit, feeling powerless. How are you feeling now?"

Marcel wasn't sure, and he didn't want to talk about it. He hooked a hand on Will's hip and dragged him closer, so close that their cocks brushed against each other. Marcel sucked in a breath and pulled again until Will was pressed against him and their legs tangled together.

"I feel like I can finally touch you, and I don't know where to start," he whispered.

"Wherever you want."

It was a lot. Marcel wanted to do everything with Will. He'd been a spirit for only a few weeks, but during those weeks, he'd believed he wouldn't come back. It had made him realize how precious life was, and Will was part of that. They might have years together, but Marcel wanted to leave his imprint on Will the way Will had left his on him.

Their lips met. They'd kissed yesterday, but it hadn't been the same. Will had been gentle. He'd made sure Marcel was okay and had taken care of him. Now, Marcel wanted to take care of Will.

He slithered down Will's body, his attention on every single movement Will made. He wanted to be sure Will enjoyed what they were doing.

Will didn't try to stop Marcel, not even when Marcel stopped in front of his cock and gently took it between his fingers. He leaned forward and inhaled deeply, Will's scent searing itself into Marcel's nose and his memory. It was a different scent than the one Will presented to everyone else, and it was solely for Marcel.

Marcel kissed the soft skin of Will's shaft. When he licked it, Will groaned and screwed his eyes shut. He reached for Marcel's hair, and Marcel was more than happy to let him hold onto him.

He grabbed Will's thigh with his free hand, his own cock with the other, and swallowed Will's. He didn't know what Will liked, but he was looking forward to finding out. In the meantime, he used every trick he knew, licking the leaking slit in the head of Will's cock, then wrapping his lips around the head and sucking.

Will's hips shot up, causing Marcel to cough. He swallowed, not wanting this to end. He was enjoying himself, and this was something he'd thought he'd lost forever.

He hadn't.

He dove onto Will's cock again and swallowed it as deeply as he could without having to pull away. He sucked hard, then pushed down again, his fingers tightening on the flesh of Will's thigh. He didn't want to hurt Will, but he hoped he'd leave bruises. He wanted Will to see them and remember this. He wanted to leave his mark on the man he'd fallen in love with when he'd thought he'd lost everything.

"I'm going to come," Will said roughly.

Marcel wanted to continue and swallow everything Will had to give him, but at the same time, he wanted more.

He let go of Will's cock, ignored his pained groan, and scrambled out of the blankets. He grabbed the pillow he'd used last night and hugged it as he settled on his knees and tilted his hips up, offering himself to Will.

It took a second for Will to understand what was going on. He rolled to his knees behind Marcel and gently touched Marcel's ass, causing Marcel to shiver.

"Are you sure?" Will asked.

"Yes. I want you to fuck me and remind me I'm alive and that I'm yours. Please."

Marcel half expected Will to try to make him change his mind, but he didn't. Instead, he parted Marcel's ass cheeks. Marcel felt him move, and the next thing he knew, something warm and wet dragged along his hole.

This wasn't what he'd meant when he'd said he wanted to feel alive, but it certainly did the trick.

Marcel arched his back in an attempt to get his ass even closer to Will's face. Will gripped Marcel's hips, keeping him in place as he slowly opened him for his cock. It felt like an eternity as Will licked, sucked, and thrust his tongue and fingers into Marcel. Marcel didn't mind. He loved sex, especially with Will, and he wanted to take his time and enjoy every single second of it.

But even his patience had its limit, and Marcel was about to reach it.

"Enough," he ground out.

Will slid his tongue out of Marcel's ass, and Marcel felt every inch of it leaving his body. "Ready?" Will croaked.

Knowing that he sounded that way because of what he'd done to Marcel was almost enough for Marcel to come. He grabbed the base of his cock and squeezed. He thought of things he'd rather not think about, like the state York was in and what Marcel wanted to do to Kurt. By the time he wasn't afraid he'd come at the slightest burst of wind, Will was pushing the head of his cock against Marcel's hole.

Marcel held his breath as it breached him. Will had made sure he was as prepped as possible, but it still burned. Marcel rejoiced in the sensation, because it was one more thing reminding him that he was still alive and that he'd made it out of the hell hole he'd been kept in.

Will didn't hesitate or slow down. He entered Marcel in one long, smooth movement, then paused to give Marcel a moment. Marcel breathed through the burning sensation and reached back blindly. When his hand touched Will's, Will linked their fingers together and pulled. Marcel's other arm felt too weak to hold him up, but he shouldn't have worried. Will leaned over his back, grabbed his other wrist, and pulled that arm back, too, locking Marcel into place.

Then he fucked Marcel.

He was forceful, not slowing down or hesitating, taking his pleasure from Marcel's body. His hips snapped, pushing his cock into Marcel's body before retreating, then pushing in again.

Marcel loved it. Will was the only person he'd trust to do this, and he reveled in it. He loved that Will was doing this to him, and it was easy to let go and follow his pleasure, since he didn't have anything else to think about. The only thing he needed to focus on was his pleasure, and he did.

He shuddered when Will's cock dragged against his prostate. Will noticed it and pushed in again, clearly intent on driving Marcel nuts — and succeeding.

Marcel cried out and stopped resisting. He hadn't been trying very hard anyway, and he trusted Will, so he let go. Will would catch him, just like he had before.

Marcel's cock twitched as the head spurted his release all over the sheets under him. Will didn't stop moving. If anything, he went faster, slammed into Marcel harder, until Marcel wondered if he'd come a second time. He didn't find out, because Will groaned, and Marcel felt his cock jerk in his body as Will filled him.

This was what Marcel hadn't wanted to lose. It had taken him almost dying to find Will, but now that he had, he wasn't giving him up. He couldn't have even if he'd wanted to.

And he didn't.

The sound of the front door slamming open made both Marcel and Will jump. They had no time to say anything before Jerome's voice reached them.

"Marcel? Where are you?" he called out.

Marcel and Will looked at each other before scrambling out of bed. Maybe if they managed to get dressed before Jerome reached them, this wouldn't be a fucking disaster.

Will should have known it would be. Why had he given his best friend a key to his apartment again?

The bedroom door opened, and Jerome stepped in. "Has Will given you his bed for the night?" he asked. "That's nice of him, but where is he?" He froze and stared at the bed.

Will had managed to get out of bed, but he hadn't been able to find his underwear, which was buried under the blankets. He'd been intent on pulling his jeans on, but he'd only managed to get one leg into the fabric.

Marcel, on the other hand, seemed to have given up trying to get dressed entirely and had wrapped the sheets and blankets around his body. He was out of breath, and Will wondered if it was because of their lovemaking or because of what had happened to him.

Jerome stared at both of them. Will had no idea how his

best friend would take the fact that he and Marcel were dating, and he wasn't sure what to say.

"Jerome?" Lindsey asked in the hallway. "Did you find them?"

Jerome continued staring. "I did," he croaked.

"Is everything okay? Do they need help?" Lindsey appeared next to Jerome, took one look into the bedroom, and started laughing. "I see. Well, they don't need help, so why don't you come with me?" He took Jerome's hand and gently led him away. "Everyone's here, and we brought breakfast," he said over his shoulder. "We'll be waiting for you in the kitchen."

He closed the door behind them, leaving Marcel and Will alone. Marcel flopped onto the mattress, laughing. "I guess this was one way to tell my brother we're together."

"Do you think he'll have a problem with it?" Will asked as he finished putting on his jeans.

"I don't see why he should. You think he'll have a problem with us being together?"

"I hope he won't, but with everything that happened, he's a bit overprotective when it comes to you."

Marcel reached for Will's hand and pulled him onto the bed. "But you won't hurt me." He kissed Will. "Besides, when you think about it, aren't you the best person for me to be with? Jerome loves you. You've been his best friend since we were kids, and he knows you inside and out. He knows the kind of person you are and that you'll treat me well. He's just shocked."

Will hoped that was the case. He didn't want to have to choose between Marcel and Jerome, and he didn't know which one he'd choose if he was forced to. He wanted to believe he'd pick Marcel, but as much as he loved him, Jerome had been his best friend for close to thirty years.

It would hurt, whoever Will ended up choosing.

But maybe he wouldn't have to. Maybe Jerome *had* just been in shock, and he'd be happy for them. If there was one good thing that had come out of this situation, it was the fact that Will and Marcel had fallen in love.

Will had to help Marcel back out of bed and into the shower, then to dress. He supported him as they slowly walked to the kitchen, and Will listened to the sound of the people gathered there. He didn't usually have a lot of people over, just Jerome. It was a huge change, but not an unpleasant one. Will hoped their little group would stay close, even now that Marcel was safe.

They walked into the kitchen, and everyone turned to them. Jerome was still staring ahead, but Lindsey was smiling and gave Will a thumbs up. Victor was sipping on what had to be a cup of tea, knowing him, and Leo was at the stove, the smell of bacon filling the room telling Will what he was cooking.

Then there was York.

Will had no idea why the guy was here, but he didn't mind. What he did mind was the fact that York seemed terrified, as if someone in the room was about to eat him. Will supposed it wasn't far-fetched, not when four of the people in the kitchen could shift into dragons, but he wanted York to feel at ease. Thankfully, Timothy was already working on that, talking to York and pushing a cup of coffee toward him. York took it with hesitant hands, but he gave Timothy a tiny smile, and Timothy smiled back.

When York leaned back, Will was surprised to see Cleo in his lap, holding on to his thigh with her claws. York winced, but he didn't push her off and instead stroked her furless head. Cleo didn't usually like people, let alone crowds, so Will hadn't expected her to be in the kitchen with everyone. He was glad she was, since it seemed to be helping York.

Will took a deep breath. These were his people, and he

hoped he'd never lose any of them, no matter how much time passed.

He guided Marcel toward one of the empty chairs and helped him sit down. "You want coffee?" he asked.

Marcel nodded. "Please. I missed it."

Will made his way to the coffee machine, bumping into Leo as he did so. Leo grinned at him, and without looking away from the bacon he was cooking, asked, "Have you been taking good care of Marcel?"

Will hoped he wasn't blushing. "As good as I could."

"Is that what shocked Jerome so badly? Because he looks like he saw a ghost, but we both know that's not possible."

"Marcel and I are working things out."

"Good. I was hoping something good would come out of all of this. God knows we're going to need it if Kurt continues trying to put together a ghostly army."

Will filled two cups with coffee, frowning as he did so. "You think he'll try again? We took away all the shifters and most of the psychics he had."

Leo shrugged. "Who knows? But people like him, who believe they've been wronged and that people need to pay for that, don't give up easily. I'm sure this is just a small setback. I wouldn't be surprised if he tried finding other ways to control ghosts."

They had everyone's attention now, so the conversation continued even once Will moved to the table to give Marcel his cup of coffee. "Is there another way he could control so many ghosts?" he asked, looking at Victor.

Victor grimaced. "There's always another way. He might kidnap more shifters and psychics, or he might use something else, maybe a magical artifact."

"Since when does magic exist?" Will asked as he slid into the chair next to Marcel's.

Marcel looked amused. "I can turn into a dragon. Are you

saying magic doesn't exist?"

Will had never thought about it that way. "I guess it does. And York said something about Kurt's girlfriend being a witch?"

Everyone turned their attention to York, who looked like he was seriously considering jumping out the window. Instead, he straightened his back and faced them. "She is, and yes, she does wield magic. I suppose she'd be able to use magical artifacts, but I don't know anything about magic."

That was something they needed to think about. "Do you think he's going to be a problem?" Will asked, hoping everyone would say no but knowing better.

Victor sighed. "I want to say no, but York knows Kurt better than anyone here. What do you think?"

York swallowed loudly. "He's not going to give up. He thinks he's owed something, and I doubt he'll stop until he gets it."

Will wished that weren't the case. "And what does he want?"

"He believes shifters shouldn't stay hidden, that you guys are better than humans. I think he said something about shifters being the next evolutionary step, or something like that. Anyway, he thinks humans should consider you gods, and I don't think anything will stop him from getting just that. This really was just a setback for him. No matter how long it takes him, he's going to try again."

Will wanted someone else to take care of this, but he doubted that would happen. He and his friends had a good idea what Kurt was up to, so they'd be the perfect people to go against him. There were eight of them, between the dragon shifters and the psychics, and Will prayed they'd be enough. He didn't want to lose anyone to Kurt, but he and the others might have to face that possibility in the future.

Kurt's plan might be ridiculous, and he might be an

arrogant idiot, but that didn't make him any less dangerous, unfortunately.

EPILOGUE

Marcel loved all of his friends, but he was glad when they finally left Will's apartment. After being unable to touch Will for so long, he wanted to spend the entire day with him in bed, resting and making love. He'd have to go back to work — if he still had a job — contact his parents, and go home to his apartment soon enough. Until then, he'd take advantage of the time he and Will had.

They flopped onto the couch as soon as the front door was closed behind Jerome, who still looked shocked, but not in a bad way. He'd taken Marcel aside for a moment to tell him he was glad to have him back in his life and that he wanted him to be happy. He hadn't said anything specific about Will, but Marcel knew it had been his way to say he was okay with Marcel and Will dating. Not that it would have changed anything if he hadn't been, but Will had been conflicted over it, so Marcel was glad it wouldn't be a problem.

"I thought they'd never leave," Will muttered.

Marcel chuckled and buried himself against Will's side. "They wanted to spend time with me and make sure I was okay. I'm sure you can understand that. You had me to yourself the entire night, but they didn't."

"I get it. I just want to spend time with you."

"I want the same." Marcel kissed Will's chest, right over his heart. "So we're a thing now?"

Will looked amused. "I suppose it depends on what you mean by a *thing*."

"I mean that we're dating. You're my boyfriend, right?"

Will's smile was blinding. "I want to be. Do you want the same?"

"That's the stupidest question I've ever heard. Of course I want to be your boyfriend."

"Good. Then, I guess you are." Will hesitated. "I know things haven't been easy for you, and we don't have to rush into this. You should take all the time you need to get used to having your life back."

This was one of the reasons Marcel had fallen in love with Will. He always thought about others before he thought about himself, and their relationship wasn't any different.

It just meant Marcel would have to think about Will before anyone else.

"What about Kurt?" Will asked.

Marcel had no answers to that question. He wanted to leave all of this behind and never see Kurt again, but he suspected he and the others would have to get involved regardless of what they wanted. "We'll deal with him when the time comes," he said.

Will nodded. "As long as you remember that you don't have to deal with him on your own. You have me and everyone else. We won't leave you alone again."

The thought that Kurt might hurt Marcel again was terrifying, but he knew that what Will was saying was true. He wasn't alone anymore. He had Will, and of course, his brother and Leo, but also Timothy and Victor, and Lindsey and York. It was strange to think he'd come out of this with more friends than he had when he'd been kidnapped, but that was what had happened, and he wouldn't lose any of them, especially not to Kurt.

It would take time for him to heal fully, and the same went for York. Hopefully, by the time Kurt was ready to strike again, they'd be ready for him. Even if they weren't, they'd face him together, just like they'd faced him together this time

ABOUT THE AUTHOR

Catherine is the creator of several series, most of them paranormal, including the Whitedell Pride Series and the Gillham Pack Series. While she graduated in translation, she decided to go the writer's way because it was more fun to create her own stories and characters.

She's been living in Italy for more than twenty years, but she's a daughter of the North—Belgium to be precise—and she misses it so much that she's already planning to move back.

She loves pizza—probably too much—her son, her pets, and of course, books. She sneaks some reading time into her schedule every time she has five minutes free from writing, demands from her various pets and son, and lastly, housework.

Connect with her:

lievens.catherine@gmail.com
BookBub: https://www.bookbub.com/authors/catherine-lievens
Website: https://authorcatherinelievens.com/
Facebook: https://www.facebook.com/catherine.lievens.9
Facebook Group: https://www.facebook.com/groups/411788002341528/
Twitter: https://twitter.com/authorCLievens
Newsletter: http://eepurl.com/c-uvKn

www.ingramcontent.com/pod-product-compliance
Lightning Source LLC
Chambersburg PA
CBHW060822120626
46557CB00001B/328